THE SINISTER CABARET

When Donald Humbie, an Edinburgh advocate in the throes of a mid-life crisis, sets off for a short break in the West Highlands, he seems only to be adding to his troubles. He soon finds himself in a hostile and threatening environment, in which inexplicable and disturbing events occur, and, worst of all, he is haunted by a malevolent troupe of strolling players led by the chameleon-like Mr Algernon Motion.

Fearing that his enemies have made off with his wife, Donald takes to the hills in search of the private detective he believes can help him solve his problems. After further bewildering adventures on the journey, at Ben Despair Lodge and the strange village of Cul an Duirn, he finally makes contact with the detective, MacNucator, who leads him on a new inner journey into his past, in search of the clues which he hopes will break the grip of his tormentors.

But Donald is not out of the woods yet . . .

In *The Sinister Cabaret* John Herdman continues the exploration of extreme states of mind, and ambiguous interior worlds, with the Gothic imagination and laconic wit which have led critics to compare him with James Hogg and R.L. Stevenson.

JOHN HERDMAN

The author was born in Edinburgh in 1941 and now lives in Highland Perthshire. Fuller biographical details and a critical appreciation can be found in Macdonald Daly's Introduction to Herdman's *Four Tales*, Zoilus Press, 2000. The author's own web site is:

www.johnherdman.co.uk

The Sinister Cabaret

John Herdman

BLACK ACE BOOKS

First published in 2001 by Black Ace Books
PO Box 6557, Forfar, DD8 2YS, Scotland

www.blackacebooks.com

© John Herdman 2001

Typeset in Scotland by Black Ace Editorial

Printed in England by Antony Rowe Ltd
Bumper's Farm, Chippenham, Wiltshire, SN14 6LH

Coda motif, fol. 191, represents: 'The waxing and waning Moon, between which runs the course of life.' Reproduced from *The Book of Signs* by Rudolf Koch.

A CIP catalogue record for this book
is available from the British Library

ISBN 1–872988–57–1

J'ai seul la clef de cette parade sauvage

Rimbaud

CONTENTS

The Journey

The Detective

What Dreams May Come

The Journey

1

A Short Break

Donald Humbie, a considerably successful advocate in his mid-fifties practising at the Scottish bar, was having a hell of a time driving along this narrow, downhill, winding, gloomy country road hemmed in by thickly planted pine trees. His neck was stiff, he felt short of breath and his steering was all to hell. There seemed to be something wrong with his car, too – a smart but unpretentious little 1998 Daewoo – though it had served him so well hitherto. The engine was roaring and screaming and protesting and the vehicle was jerking and veering wildly from side to side. His terror of those who were pursuing him was now matched by his horror at his own reckless driving and mounting fear of his seemingly uncontrollable car.

Then it flashed into his head that all this could be explained by the circumstance that he was in fact reversing, at great speed, looking over his left shoulder. When he had backed precipitately out of the forest track in the certain knowledge that they were close behind him, it had struck him that he would be wasting precious time by stopping to change into forward gear, so he had just shot off backwards down this desperately narrow, steeply declining, treacherous country road, without further thought.

What a thing to do! – even in those circumstances. This autumn holiday was not going so well.

He had left Edinburgh only a couple of days before. It wasn't his usual time for a break, the courts were sitting, but – well, really it was on doctor's orders. He wasn't exactly ill; but he certainly wasn't well either. Madeleine said it was the male menopause. She knew he needed to be off on his own for a bit, and the truth was that really she would be glad enough to see the back of him. Allowing each other their own space, that's what it was called nowadays. Things had not been so good lately, between Madeleine and himself. But then they had not been so good within himself either. He acknowledged that. And when things are not right within yourself, it follows that they can't be right with other people.

One evening recently he had been sitting in his study, putting off the work that badly needed to be done, and staring at his oldest and most faithful friends, the multifarious books on his crammed shelves, consciously willing them to explain what was wrong. The answer must be there, surely, somewhere among all those words.

'How extraordinary,' he thought, 'that I have read all the books on those shelves, bristling with ideas and life, and they have all passed through me and become part of me, yet here I sit without an idea in my head or an emotion in my heart, dead as a doornail! Something will have to be done.'

The only thing he could come up with, though, was the thought that he must 'get away for a bit', which was not really very imaginative. And that was part of the trouble: he wasn't in a very imaginative frame of mind. But he decided that's what he would do anyway; he'd go away for a few days. Then, on the morning of his departure, he didn't feel so well. He was in the bathroom when he was suddenly overcome by a deathly faintness and nausea, the sweat broke out on his brow and the world was running away from him. He sat down on the toilet seat and put his head between his knees, but for a little while he was not aware of what was going on and perhaps he even briefly lost consciousness. Then there was a curiously unnerving sense, for a moment, that he was travelling between two modes of existence and could experience both simultaneously. But it passed and he felt better, if rather strange and in an odd way detached from himself. A little shaken, he continued with his preparations for departure.

Then something else rather strange happened. He had already packed the car and was ready to set off and was saying goodbye to Madeleine when he quite unexpectedly felt very emotional and even thought that he was going to cry. He had his hands over his wife's hips.

She said in a far-away voice, 'I dreamt last night of the guillotine. They were going to execute me. It made an awful mess of me here.' She raised both her hands and rested her fingers on the back of the neck. '*You* should have done it,' she whispered. 'You would have made a cleaner job of it.'

He was going to ask, 'They — who were they?' but before he could do so she kissed him passionately. Neither of them said anything more; Donald hesitated a moment, then he turned and left.

He thought he would head for the north-west. Something was niggling away at the back of his mind. Partly it was those strange words of Madeleine's; but there was something else too. Had he failed to pack something vital? He racked his brains but couldn't pinpoint anything. Yet the further he drove the more strongly did the troubling sense assert itself — a sense which he now realized had always been there but which up till now he had successfully repressed — that he was missing something. Not something in his luggage but something in his life. It wasn't some large elusive generality like success, or fulfilment, or love, or God. Actually, he believed that he had some of those things, to some degree. No, what he was missing was something absolutely concrete and specific — something he had once had. He ought to be able to see it; he could almost touch it. Yet always it evaded him; it was just beyond reach.

That first night he had spent in a little hotel in Benderloch. The drive had been pleasant, the early autumn weather clear and fresh, he was enjoying being by himself, and but for that odd niggle at the back of his mind everything seemed to be all right. But as he dressed for dinner in his single room with the double bed he began to feel lonely and to wish that Madeleine were with him after all. The feeling was naturally accentuated as he dined by himself, the only lone diner in the restaurant. He drank a bottle of wine with his meal, which he felt was rather too much for one.

Perhaps as a result of this over-indulgence, on an impulse he decided to phone Madeleine after dinner, and ask her to join him at their old haunt of Fliuchary within the next day or two. He went up to his bedroom to get this done before his coffee arrived in the lounge. There was the familiar pause and faint click indicating an answering machine, then a male voice speaking in a guttural Eastern European accent intoned:

'You have reached the residence of Attila the Hun. I am sorry that I am unable to take your call at present, but if you care to leave your name and address, I will arrange to have you torn apart by wild horses as soon as possible. Please speak slowly after the tone.'

Dammit! – wrong number. He tried again. The same thing happened; but this time, after the voice had delivered its instructions, it laughed, quite briefly. The laugh was not a kindly one.

Well, that was not encouraging.

Donald decided to have a brandy with his coffee. What was he to do now? He really did want Madeleine to join him as soon as possible; he was almost sure of that. But how was he to get in touch with her when there was this problem with the phone? Then he remembered that he had his notebook computer with him. E-mail – that was the answer. Technology was a wonderful thing.

'Darling, I'm missing you. I'm in Benderloch tonight but going on to Fliuchary tomorrow. I'll stay there for at least a couple of days – why don't you come up and join me? I need you. I'll be at Tigh-na-Coille as usual. There seems to be a problem with the phone (ours, I mean). Love, *H.*'

H. stood for Madeleine's pet name for Donald, which it really wouldn't be fair to either of them to reveal. He posted the message and everything seemed to be fine. Technology was a great comfort.

When he checked the next morning there was as yet no reply from Madeleine. Probably she had not yet checked herself; she wouldn't have been expecting to hear from him that way. He was confident there would be a response from her by evening. Or she might just decide to give him a surprise by arriving unannounced – that would be like her. He could see now the expression of childlike pleasure – a mute 'Look, here I am!' – she would assume as she waited for his mouth to open in joyful surprise. She still had that innocent freshness.

All the same, Donald felt rather depressed as he set off on the longish haul up to Fliuchary; or not so much depressed as disorientated. 'It's one of those days when everything's different,' he said to himself. It was a feeling with which he had been familiar since childhood, though he didn't experience it very often nowadays. A sense of unfamiliarity within the familiar; everything was really the same, yet it contained within it an alienation that was imperceptible to the senses, as if the substance of the world had been infiltrated by something subversive and nothing was any longer truly as it appeared. It was usually brought on by some dislocating event, a kind of *Verfremdungseffekt*. No doubt on this occasion it was that bizarre message on the answering machine which had sparked this sense of strangeness. Who the devil could have been playing around with their phone?

He wondered whether Ken had been round to see Madeleine after he'd left. Ken was Madeleine's much younger

half-brother, and a great practical joker. A complete buf-
foon, in Donald's opinion. Yes, that was doubtless the
explanation.

All the same the feeling had not entirely dispersed
when, around half-past five, he arrived at Fliuchary at
the end of his long drive and pulled up at the familiar
guest-house. Tigh-na-Coille – almost home from home.
Donald and Madeleine had been coming here now for
about fifteen years and the welcome was always the
same. Here, at least, nothing would have changed. The
whitewashed house, the two little lawns of coarse grass
on either side of the pebbly path, the neat flower beds
under the front windows, the sea-shells arranged around
the porch, and the big stone roller for the lawn in its little
niche. His feet crunched on the pebbles. He pulled the
old-fashioned bell.

A man in his mid-forties who looked a bit like Clark
Gable, dressed in a canary waistcoat under a loudly
checked tweed suit, opened the door almost at once,
as if he had been waiting for Donald, and stared at
him impassively without speaking, a slight smirk on his
features.

'Is Mrs Macrae about?' asked Donald, with an attempt
at brightness.

'Mrs Macrae's dead,' said the man. 'I'm Mr Motion.'

'Dead? Mrs Macrae's dead? When? What happened?'

'A little over a year ago, I believe. I don't know the
details. We took over in May. I think you'll find that
everything's much as it was. Are you coming in?'

This man didn't seem to think that it should matter to
Donald that Mrs Macrae was dead! Clutching his bag,
he staggered rather than walked over the threshold, not

knowing what else to do, close to fainting with shock but already trying to steady his spirit to withstand the onflow of grief which must soon cascade over it. He followed the man up the stairs and into the familiar bedroom.

Yes, everything was much the same – in fact, absolutely the same. So much the same that it was positively obscene. Not only the décor and furnishings, even down to the bedspread, but all Mrs Macrae's things, her little personal touches, yes, actually the family photographs too! Donald wondered whether the man was playing some kind of nasty practical joke on him, whether Mrs Macrae had just popped down to the post office and this unpleasant guest had taken it upon himself to show the new arrival to his room. But then he noticed one unfamiliar object: on the dressing-table stood a large, tasteless colour photograph of a rather vulgar-looking, heavily made-up woman with a cold smile, gazing at the camera through blue, narrowed lids.

'Mrs Motion,' said the man, observing that Donald was looking at it. 'You'll have the pleasure of getting acquainted with her later.' There was something naggingly familiar about his voice.

Donald grunted non-committally. *Some pleasure!* he thought. What a piece of effrontery, to imagine that his paying guests would want to have Mrs Motion gazing upon their intimate lives throughout their stay! As soon as the man had gone he removed the photograph from the dressing-table and placed it face-down on the floor beside the waste-paper basket. He sat down on the bed, not wanting to stay, wanting in fact very much to leave. But Madeleine might well come. He got out the Toshiba; still no reply to his message. Well then, he would have to wait, and there was no saying how long. He knew that if Madeleine did come, she wouldn't want to stay here now. How shocked she would be! – not only at Mrs Macrae's totally unexpected death (she was a fit and healthy little woman, not yet 70), but at this disgusting usurpation of her home, almost of her life. How on earth could it have happened? She had a family – a daughter in Glasgow and a son somewhere in England. How could they have allowed this creature to take over their family home, wholesale, down to the last button? It wasn't canny.

But what was he to do? He could try phoning again, he supposed, but . . . somehow he didn't want to. To tell the truth, he was scared. He didn't want to hear again the voice of Attila the Hun. The voice . . . Oh, God, the voice, the voice! *That* was why Motion's voice seemed familiar! The room began to swim before his eyes: he had to lie down on the bed, and perhaps even momentarily lost consciousness once again.

When he had recovered a little he stood up and a convulsion of rage coursed through his spirit. He wanted to confront Motion at once and shout '*Impostor!*' at him at the top of his voice. For that was all he was – a wretched, vulgar impostor!

Donald ran down the stairs and found the man in the private sitting room, reading a newspaper. He stood in the doorway for a moment, uncertain whether the other even knew he was there; then, instead of what he intended, he merely said:

'I'll be eating out this evening.'

'That's a sensible decision,' replied Mr Motion, without even looking up from his newspaper. 'We don't serve evening meals.'

Utterly wrong-footed, Donald stood there awkwardly for another moment then left the house and walked quickly down the road. He felt as if he knew he had been infected with some deadly disease but was still in the incubation period, waiting with unutterable dread for the first symptoms to appear. In the meantime he had to carry on living because there was simply nothing else to be done, but it had all become meaningless. He walked on in the steadily encroaching twilight. The little details of life had taken on a feverish intensity. Ahead of him an old gentleman was irritatedly flicking litter off the pavement with inept, jerky movements of his walking-stick.

'That's me in twenty years' time,' he thought fleetingly. As Donald overtook him the old man turned sharply and looked at him and he was – just that. Himself in twenty years. To see one's double – wasn't that supposed to portend approaching death?

2

The Rag-Doll

When Donald got back to his room later that evening after a bar meal in the hotel, the picture of Mrs Motion had been returned to its place on the dressing-table. He had not yet laid eyes on her in the flesh, nor had there been any sign of her husband when he got in. He was doing his best to blot the whole thing out of his consciousness. He went straight to bed, though without in his heart of hearts expecting to sleep.

But the unexpected was what happened: he was asleep almost before his head had touched the pillow.

If it could be called sleep. For immediately he was assailed by atrocious images, lascivious nightmares. They all concerned Mrs Motion; or it might be better to say that they consisted in a protracted assault on the part of Mrs Motion upon his body and his soul. But the fearful thing was that in these dreams Madeleine, his dear wife Madeleine, the love of his life, for whom he had served twice seven years, or damn near it, was confused, confounded, with the hideous vamp, Mrs Motion! Mrs Motion would put her arms around him, kiss him, seduce him, and he had to succumb because he *knew* that she was really Madeleine. 'It *is* me,' she insisted. 'You know it is!' And Donald replied – meaning it, too – 'Yes, I know . . . I know your body.' They kissed passionately and Donald began pulling Mrs Motion's clothes off and making love to her standing up against a wall.

Then it seemed to the dreamer that he was awake and that Motion himself had come into the bedroom and was standing in front of the dressing-table watching all this going on. 'I told you that you two would be getting acquainted later on,' he observed smugly, smiling and nodding his head in approval. But Donald no longer had the heart to make love in these circumstances and he felt his sex turning to mush. 'Well, that's good,' said Mr Motion, 'because I've come to offer you a part in a pantomime, my dear.' Madeleine – for the woman was now clearly his wife again – was all eagerness and immediately lost every shred of interest in Donald as she turned her attention towards this meretricious impresario. It was true, too, that in real life Madeleine took part in amateur dramatics. Donald was at once in a frenzy of jealousy but he was completely paralysed and could do nothing to change matters. The dream faded and altered, and after a little it seemed to the advocate – he was really convinced of it – that Madeleine, now once more in the form of Mrs Motion, was performing fellatio upon him as he lay still paralysed, unable to move so much as his little finger, and that Motion was watching it all from just outside the bedroom door.

But at last the dreams ended and after that Donald had
two or three hours of sound sleep. It was after nine when
he awoke. However bad things have been at night they
always seem better in the morning, and he was actually
ready for his breakfast. He dressed, washed and shaved
rapidly, saying to himself as he did so that he was no
longer going to take all this lying down; he was going to
take matters into his own hands and let the Motions know
that they could not get away with just anything. Exactly
what he was going to say he wasn't sure, but the occasion
would tell him.

When he opened the door he nearly tripped over a tray.
On the tray lay a plate with a couple of slices of burnt,
leathery toast, a single portion of wrapped butter and
a single individual marmalade; and a chipped Mickey
Mouse mug of tea with a scum of milk on the surface,
clearly stone-cold. This was too much. Donald purposely
stood on the plate and kicked over the mug (after all, it was
mere luck that he had looked down when he stepped out of
the door) and, rage in his heart, stormed downstairs. But
there was no-one about at all, not in the sitting room or
the dining room or the kitchen; the house was as deserted
as the *Marie Celeste*.

He managed to get a late breakfast in the hotel and then
found a public telephone. With his heart in his mouth
he dialled the number of the house in India Street. The
answering machine was once more on; but this time the
voice of Motion said only:

'This is no longer the residence of Donald Humbie,
Q.C.'

When he had laid down the receiver, Donald Humbie,
Q.C. held his head in his hands for a few moments, trem-

bling from head to foot. Then he set off walking wherever his feet chose to carry him.

By the time he returned to Tigh-na-Coille in the early afternoon he had made up his mind that the only thing to do was to call the police. This was no mere practical joke: he was convinced that Madeleine was in danger. What it all meant he couldn't even begin to put together. The disreputable Motions had somehow invaded the very fabric of his life like an insidious illness, but how or why it was impossible to imagine. He had no doubt at all that it was Motion's voice on the answering machine; but how could he have got to Edinburgh and back to put it there, in the time since Donald had left? At first he had thought the best course of action would be to drive back home at once to see if Madeleine was safe – but suppose she were not there? Suppose she should arrive here after he had set off and be delivered into the clutches of that corrupt couple?

No, no, he must at all costs get to the nearest police station at the earliest moment. How he would set about explaining the bizarre business so as to convey its real seriousness and moment, or even be believed, even be confident of convincing the police that he wasn't crazy . . . well, he would have to cross that bridge when he came to it.

But he had to get there fast.

Motion was standing at the front door of Tigh-na-Coille – dreadful to think that it was the very same house which had welcomed them so often and so warmly – puffing affectedly at a cheroot in the hazy afternoon sunshine.

'Ah, Mr Humbie!' he exclaimed expansively, all his sardonic manner gone. 'Your wife arrived about an hour ago. She was tired after the journey – said she was going to lie down and take a rest.'

'Oh! – that's wonderful!' Donald's heart leapt with joy and relief, the nightmare instantly dissolved. He positively beamed at the tasteless proprietor as he slipped past him to run eagerly up the stairs. He keeked through the door so as not to disturb Madeleine too soon: he wanted to sneak up and plant a little kiss on her cheek before she knew he was there. Yes, there she was under the duvet, her face turned away from him, her lovely rich brown hair – one of her very best features – spread a little over the pillow behind her. He tiptoed over, bent and pulled back the edge of the duvet to reveal the lovely soft cheek on which he was to plant the kiss, and . . . oh God, oh God, that ever this should be! . . . saw that what was lying in the bed was a life-size rag-doll.

It is impossible to convey adequately what must have been Donald's feelings at that moment as, bending gently down to reunite himself lovingly with the wife whom he had feared the victim of sinister and nefarious wrong-doing, but who now appeared to be so unexpectedly and joyfully restored to him, he discovered in her place a hideous, mocking parody, a lifeless simulacrum whose dead eyes stared back at his with a blank gaze that nullified love and blasted hope; and found himself certain, beyond the possibility of error, that the hair glued wig-like to that gruesome skull had only hours before been the crowning glory of his wife's deeply cherished living frame. Who can hope to render that experience with decency or discretion? No, to pry into the inner impressions of a sensate being at such a crisis would be a presumption which one could not hold justified by even the most pressing imperative of realism.

Enough, then to observe that after gazing open-mouthed at that indecent dummy for some moments, frozen to the spot and held vice-like in the steely grip of those emotions which we have not dared to analyse, and after stretching out his hand to touch the hair and disturbing it enough to reveal at the back of the neck a split in the material through which oozed something which resembled dried-up turkey stuffing, Donald turned his back upon the hideous thing, threw into his bag those few items which he had unpacked the night before, and bolted down the stairs and out the front door as fast as his legs would carry him. As he did so mingled peels of mocking laughter – two, male and female – issued from the house: not from any one source but with a stereophonical effect, as if it were the house itself which had taken on the personalities of its detestable inmates and was laughing out loud with their common voice.

Donald Humbie leapt into his car and drove off like the wind in the direction of Achnasheen. He had no idea where he was headed, his only thought was to get away and put a limitless distance between himself and the horrors behind him. But almost at once he had the impression that he was being followed. At first it was only a sixth sense that seemed to warn him, but after two or three miles he did indeed spy in his rear-view mirror, not so very far behind him, a black Range Rover which he now remembered having seen parked at the side of Tigh-na-Coille. Frantically he sought for a means to throw his pursuers off. Taking advantage of a slight bend which hid him from their view, he precipitately swung right into a side road which he didn't remember ever having noticed before, although he had been familiar with the area for years.

The road climbed twisting into a high moorland beyond which lay heavily forested hills. After a mile or two he began to think that his ruse had been successful, until he reached a high point from which he could see the road winding up below him – and there was the Range Rover, perhaps closer behind him than it had ever been. He drove on, desperately searching for a haven, until the road entered thick pine woods. After half a mile he saw an opening on his left, an old forestry track now partly grown over but still capable of admitting a car, and drove up it for fifty yards or so until it became impassable.

He could still be seen from the road if one was looking, but he must just hope that the Range Rover would sweep past without noticing him. He waited, his eyes glued to the mirror, but it never came. Had it given up the pursuit? Surely not! No, they must have realized what he had done and were playing cat-and-mouse with him, waiting for him to re-emerge to find them right there on his tail! Donald was seized by an ungovernable panic. It was then that he lost his head completely, backed down the track and on to the road, and continued driving down it in reverse like a madman, utterly in the grip of unreason.

3

At Cant's Hotel

Donald realized that he had to get a grip. He was not doing himself any good by giving way to panic like this. At the first opportunity – for the road itself was too narrow to turn in – he wheeled the car round and proceeded in the direction he had been travelling, but in forward gear. There was no sign of the pursuing vehicle. The forest was bearing down upon him oppressively on every side, but after a few miles it began to thin out, and then he was looking down on a village lying deep in a glen through which ran a substantial, fast-moving burn. He had certainly never been here before and was quite puzzled as to where he could be.

As he drove down into the settlement he saw no name sign; it struck him that the feel of the place was not very Scottish, rather it had something of a Middle-European character; the surrounding hills, too, looked almost Alpine. But the names on the rather old-fashioned-looking shops were certainly Scottish: he noticed Chisholm, Mac-pherson, Catanach. There were few people about. The road dropped down to a hump-backed bridge then, doubling sharply back, opened into a little square. On the left stood a low, rambling building with the name 'Cant's Hotel' in gold letters over the entrance. What was it that made him instinctively dislike that name? No matter. Donald parked the car and went in.

It seemed not much different from many small Scottish country hotels. There was a brass bell on the reception desk: the kind that one banged to summon attention. So Donald banged it and waited. No-one came. He peered into the sitting-room and the bar, which opened off oppo-site sides of the entrance hall, but both were deserted, so he went up the steep spiral staircase with its worn maroon carpet and long-unpolished brass handrail. Upstairs there was a long corridor with an uneven, creaking floor. All the bedrooms he looked into were devoid of furniture but the floors were covered uniformly with thick dark-brown carpets and the walls were freshly painted. There were signs that new plumbing had been installed, and possibly some new bathrooms. Donald concluded that the hotel was probably closed for renovation and that he had only been able to get in because the owners were about some-where, or possibly workmen.

He went into one of the rooms and was suddenly over-come by intense weariness: if only there had been a bed! He shut the door behind him. This room had a tiny bath-room in which the WC sat on a raised platform. With a feeling of pleasurable secretiveness and mild guilt he lay down on the luxuriously new carpet with his head on this platform as a pillow, and after arranging his sweater under him to cushion his hip, fell almost at once into a profound sleep.

When he woke it was already dusk. He was stiff and a bit cold, but what made him shiver was a dream he had had. In fact it was less a dream than a vivid memory which had come back to him in sleep, scarcely modified except by that visionary, other-worldly atmosphere peculiar to dreams. It dated back to a time when he was about ten and attending a school in which a clique of bullies maintained power through a permanent reign of terror. This gang was led by a quite small and insignificant boy who, however, was able to dominate others, including many much larger and tougher than himself, through the powerful sway of his depraved and probably psychotic personality. In the dream memory this person was whipping with bramble stalks a small boy stripped to the waist and hung by his ankles from the branch of an ash tree, while the rest of the gang stood around and cheered him on.

The leader's name was Cant.

Alone and friendless in a strange, empty hotel in the autumn gloaming, in an unknown place far from home, tricked and cozened and pursued by sinister ruffians who he feared had kidnapped or harmed or even done away with his dear wife . . . it is not to be wondered at that Donald felt depressed and anxious. He needed to find and speak to a sympathetic human being. He moved cautiously to the door and made his way down the corridor to the stair, guided by a dim light from downstairs. There was still no-one about, so he went through a green baize door which opened off a niche beside the reception desk. The room he entered was in darkness, but at the farther end a sliver of light showed beneath another door. He groped his way towards it, bumping into furniture. On the other side there was a good deal of noise, thumping and scraping of chairs, but no sound of human voices. He opened the door an inch and peeked through apprehensively.

Before his eyes was a large, barn-like function room with rows of long tables covered with white tablecloths. Around these tables were seated fifty or sixty people conversing volubly in sign language. There was a general air of excitement and expectation among these assembled deaf-mutes, and every now and again one of them would point or gesticulate towards the curtained stage at the far end of the hall. Evidently some kind of performance was shortly due to begin.

Meanwhile two or three girls were serving the audience plates of sandwiches and jugs of Irn-Bru. Donald was by this time ravenously hungry, having eaten nothing since breakfast-time, and the sight of the food was enough to overcome his nervousness and persuade him to slip into the function room. Trying to look as unobtrusive and mute as possible, he made his way to a smaller table at the side where some of the ashets of sandwiches had been left, and, grabbing hold of a plate, loaded it with food and began stuffing himself unceremoniously.

No-one paid him the slightest attention.

Donald retreated with his plate to the near end of the table closest to the door by which he had entered, where nobody was sitting, and sat surreptitiously devouring his sandwiches and refreshing himself with Irn-Bru while he waited to see what was about to happen. It was approaching seven-thirty. The sense of expectation among the audience became more marked, and what might by analogy be described as a hush began to overtake the silent conversations which were being carried on. Then the lights dimmed, plates were pushed aside and all turned towards the stage in pleasurable anticipation.

The curtains parted – old-fashioned maroon plush curtains which reminded Donald of the pantomimes of his childhood – and a kind of firework display ensued, no doubt simulated, which ultimately resolved itself into the words THE SINISTER CABARET in bright, gaudy colours, red and green and blue and orange and mauve. When this had dissolved, the Master of Ceremonies entered with a crude swagger: a strutting, posturing circus ringmaster with a top hat, boots and spurs, and carrying a whip which he cracked from time to time just for the sake of it. Beneath the fancy dress and the make-up of this vulgarian Donald had little difficulty in recognizing the person of the odious Motion! Oh, dear God!

The compère now wordlessly introduced his co-players: his wife, scantily attired in a figure-hugging black costume with suspenders and fishnet stockings, and an older man in a tramp's outfit whom, with a profound sinking of the heart, Donald at once pinpointed as the sadistic torturer Cant whose appearance – though forty-odd years had naturally altered it – his recent dream had vividly restored to his memory. And there was someone else he recognized: Cant's brutal lieutenant from those far-off days, a great hulking oaf known by the nickname Scrote. In the course of the act which followed he came to realize something else: this Scrote was the very same individual whom he had successfully prosecuted for embezzlement some years before, not long after he had taken silk, without ever identifying him as his childhood tormentor.

The audience was already ecstatic, although almost nothing had so far happened, and what had was sadly commonplace stuff: the excitement was really quite silly and childish and unjustified. The performance took the form of a series of sketches played in mime but introduced by one or other of the actors with a short verse which supposedly rehearsed its subject-matter but often seemed only marginally related to what actually happened. These verses were spoken out loud but mouthed with exaggerated and ponderous articulation so that they could be lip-read by the deaf-mutes, who of course found them hysterically funny. Actually they were uniformly banal and often in execrable taste. This, for instance:

> *The budgie old sat in the cold*
> *And whistled a rotten tune.*
> *A butcher's lad said, 'Christ, that's bad!'*
> *And squashed him with a spoon.*

This was played as a pantomime skit with Mrs Motion playing the poor budgie and the sadist Scrote the reprehensible butcher's boy. Sometimes there was a feeble attempt at profundity and *double-entendre*:

> *There once was a burrowless bunny*
> *Who caught a chill and died.*
> *'Oh, boo-hoo-hoo!' said Auntie,*
> *'But better than dying inside!'*

The audience roared with laughter at this, although it was very doubtful whether they had understood it. They were one of those exasperating audiences who laugh simply because they are on a day out and have to be seen to be enjoying themselves, and also out of a desire to be seen to be knowing. Donald had had quite enough of this show and was just thinking of sneaking out again by the way he had come when a truly dreadful development occurred. The detestable Motion declaimed a new verse:

> *A kiss or two, a ray of love:*
> *You said you must be on your way.*
> *Although we'll never meet again,*
> *A face to recognize some day.*

—and then a new actress appeared on the stage, a woman with a lithe figure and long, rich-brown hair, a woman whom Donald knew only too well. It was Madeleine – or her double. The same, in fact, in every feature, every tiniest detail, yet Donald knew in his heart of hearts that it was not his wife.

And now – horror of horrors! – he saw played out before his eyes his parting from his wife a couple of days before (though it seemed now to belong to another lifetime), with his own part taken by the indecent Cant. Everything was the same, including – and this was played with peculiar emphasis – the moment when Madeleine had related her dream and indicated the place where the guillotine had made a mess of her neck. Cold sweat broke out on him. When the sketch was over Motion sauntered back on stage and remarked:

'Nice one, eh?' as if addressing Donald personally.

After that the Madeleine substitute kept appearing in sketches that were obscene, sordid, suggestive or depraved, usually as some character whose innocence was hideously debauched by a villain played by Cant. Donald now found himself unable to leave, though he longed to do so, held in a hypnotic, humiliating, trance-like state by the silly, catchy jingles:

> *The Leith Police dismisseth us*
> *As oftentimes before,*
> *And thoroughly off that pisseth us*
> *As they show us to the door.*

> * * * *

> *Home, home on the scheme*
> *Where the pit-bull and Rottweiler scream,*
> *Where seldom is heard an encouraging word*
> *But the drugs make it seem like a dream.*

It was all odious and reprehensible, and Donald, terrified in truth to the roots of his being, experienced a violent desire to take it out on the deaf-mutes for their complicity, to rage among them, overturning their tables and throwing their food around for endorsing all this evil play-acting and imposture. But at last it seemed that the show was coming to an end. The players assembled all together on the stage for what appeared to be a finale, and sang in turns and finally in unison the lines of a farewell ditty:

Nothing is quite the way it seems:
The Sinister Cabaret corrupts your dreams.
What you were and you would have been,
What you would rather remained unseen:
Nasty longings and hidden gall—
The Sinister Cabaret reveals them all.
You want to escape and disappear
But the Sinister Cabaret is always here:
In your attic and in your bed—
The Sinister Cabaret is inside your head.

The curtain dropped to tumultuous applause and then rose again and the players strutted and bowed and linked hands and grinned away with infamous self-satisfaction while the mutes rose from their seats and raised their clapping hands above their heads and made uncouth noises of appreciation. Fury had now quite driven out Donald's fear, and the enraged advocate pushed forward between the tables jostling the audience out of his way and leapt up onto the stage.

'Where is my wife? What have you done to her?' he shouted at Motion, striding right up to him with clenched fists.

Motion smiled patronizingly. 'What have we done to her? What have *you* done to her, that's the question!'

'Can't you see that she's one of us now?' asked the Motion woman, mockingly.

The Madeleine-substitute gave Donald a pitying look and held her hands out wide as if to indicate her helplessness.

'Don't give me that! Are you saying I don't know my own wife? I know an impostor when I see one. What have you done to her?'

He grabbed Motion by the collar and twisted. 'And what did you mean by placing that wretched mammet in my bed?'

Cant now walked up to Donald menacingly.

'I think you ought to go now,' he said.

'You filthy little shit!' said Donald. 'I think I'll kill you quite soon. Yes, I think I'll do that.'

Cant made as if he was going to hit Donald, but Donald grabbed hold of a belaying-pin which was lying nearby and he quickly retreated a step or two. God knows why there should be a belaying-pin lying nearby, it flashed through Donald's mind, but there is usually one around when it is needed, either that or a marline-spike: he supposed it must have been used in one of the sketches. But what more could Donald do? A wave of mingled despair and contempt swept over him and he turned on his heel and left the stage. Then he was once more convulsed by rage and he turned back towards the troupe and shouted:

'Frauds! Impostors! Actors!'

But they just laughed. The deaf-mutes, the wind now completely out of their sails, parted silently (of course) to let him past, and he left the hall by the way he had come. He re-entered the entrance hall of the hotel, went upstairs and groped his way to the bedroom he had occupied earlier. Feeling suddenly as overcome by weariness as if he had been drugged, he staggered into the bathroom, lay down in a foetal position and was instantly asleep.

In spite of a deeply disturbed night, haunted by vile and confused images which he could no longer remember clearly, Donald awoke the next morning in a determined, almost a defiant mood, and sat on the floor with his hands around his knees trying to think of a way forward.

'A plan – I must think of a plan!'

He supposed that the sensible thing would be to go to the police, but the police were an unimaginative bunch on the whole, and he had, he realized, nothing very concrete to tell them; indeed, no evidence at all of criminal or even illegal activity. The story he had to tell was odd in the extreme and he was well aware that he risked not being taken seriously. There was his professional status, of course, but up here he was unknown; and besides he felt somehow in a different world, in which none of his quotidian assumptions held good. Still, he couldn't think of any course of action that seemed to offer better prospects of success.

Donald looked at his watch: it was just after eight and there was no sound of life at all in the hotel. He went over to the window and looked out cautiously. There were few people about. The atmosphere here is strange, he thought; but he couldn't put his finger on the nature of the strangeness. There were shops in the village, anyway, and by this time at least one of them ought to be open.

He bought some food in the general store and leaned against the wall of the bridge over the burn while he had a couple of rolls and a carton of milk for his breakfast. It was nearly October but the weather was holding; there was a freshness in the air, a kind of suspended quality in the atmosphere, as if the earth were waiting for something to happen. What? There was a strangeness, certainly, in which he couldn't quite find his way, but he couldn't say in what it consisted. It was a bit like the way one saw the world in early childhood.

He felt drawn to Chisholm's shop, on the opposite side of the square from the general store and sauntered across. It seemed if anything to be a hardware store, but not in the normal sense. As well as the usual things such a place might have, it was crammed with all kinds of obsolete goods and equipment such as would have been necessary in a traditional rural society of seventy-five or a hundred years ago: harnesses, gear for carriages, agricultural implements and materials for all kinds of traditional arts and crafts. In a way it was like a museum, but there was a sense that these things were still needed and used. All was orderly, adequate, satisfying. Behind the counter was an elderly man who fitted his shop in every respect.

'Good morning,' said Donald. 'Could you tell me where the nearest police station is, please? None here, I suppose?'

'Oh, goodness, no. The nearest would be . . . maybe Ullapool. Yes, probably Ullapool. What would you be wanting with the polis?'

Donald was a bit taken aback by the directness of this, but the question was asked in a friendly manner, and this was the first person he'd come across since he left home who he felt was sympathetic enough for him to confide in. He leaned forward confidentially.

'The truth is . . . Do you know that cabaret act that was on in Cant's Hotel last night?'

'Oh, ay?' said the old man in a discreet, non-committal tone.

'Well, I've been having a bit of trouble with them over the past day or two. I'd rather not go into the details,

but . . . well, to tell you the truth, I've reason to suppose that they're up to no good. Don't repeat that, mind
you . . . '

'No, no. I'll keep quiet, right enough.'

'I can't say for sure that it's a police matter, but I think
they ought to know.'

'You'd be better with the detective,' said the old man
decisively.

'There's a detective? Where?' Donald immediately felt
that he would be much more comfortable dealing with the
detective.

The shopkeeper said a name in Gaelic which Donald
couldn't take in.

'It's a fifty-mile drive,' he said with a shake of the
head and a slight chuckle, 'but as the crow flies it's no
more than a quarter of that.'

An idea suddenly occurred to Donald. He would be
better off without the car: he couldn't then be pursued
by that black Range Rover. He would feel more secure
out there on his own, reliant on his own wits.

'Is it walkable?'

'Oh ay. If you're fit, sir, you could walk it no bother.'

'Could you show it to me on a map – do you have a
map of the area for sale?'

The old man shook his head again, as if enjoying some
private joke. He was one of those old Highland people
who seem perpetually, though not unkindly, amused by
the naiveté and childishness of the city-bred.

'No, no. No maps, sir. But I could draw you one myself,
right enough.'

'That would be very kind.'

The old man disappeared to the back of the shop and

shortly re-emerged with a large sheet of brown wrapping-paper and a thick-nibbed fountain pen. He set to work with great concentration, his tongue protruding a little between his teeth, and every now and again giving a little grunt. His draughtsmanship was firm and workmanlike.

'Tell me about this detective,' said Donald as the old man put the finishing touches to the map. 'I'm surprised that there is enough work to support him in these parts.'

'Oh, he doesn't do it for the money, sir. He does it for the love of the thing. He's just a man, you see, who loves detecting.'

'And he's good at it, is he?'

'None better.' The old man bent down and rummaged under the counter, coming up after a minute with a worn and grubby card bearing the legend:

PETER MacNUCATOR
Private Detective
Cul an Duirn 212

'Thank you,' said Donald. 'I'm most grateful. I'd better buy some stuff for my journey, I suppose.'

The old man extended his hand with quiet pride towards his plentiful stock.

'It's all here, sir. This is all you need.'

Donald bought a small backpack and a number of other items which he reckoned he might need. He asked the old man if he would be kind enough to keep an eye on his car while he was gone, and was advised to park it in front of the hardware store. He thanked the old man for his trouble.

'My prayers go with you,' said the strange old fellow.

Donald went back to the other shop to buy provisions for his journey, then went to the car to transfer what he needed from his bag to the backpack. The hotel still looked deserted and there was no sign at all of the Sinister Cabaret.

It was around nine o' clock when he set off.

4

Ben Despair Lodge

Donald left the village in the opposite direction from that of his arrival and found the track indicated on the old man's map. The Chisholm trail, he thought, that's what I'm on. Soon it was following the course of a burn which must flow into the river which the village straddled. The traveller found himself in a delightful little glen, very enclosed, which climbed steeply into the wildly impressive hills above to the north-east. The banks of the glen were clothed with heather and bracken and scattered with alders and many rowan trees, whose luxuriant deep-red berries were now in full flush. There was a feeling of beauty and repose, of richness of experience, which Donald found deeply satisfying. His mood lightened, too; the mission to the detective had given him a sense of purpose, of hope that he would no longer be struggling alone and without effect against an enemy he could scarcely identify and whose objectives he did not understand.

In this way he went on happily for about an hour, climbing all the time on a rocky little path which required his full attention if he were to keep his footing. As he climbed, though, the environment became gradually less friendly. The vegetation thinned out and eventually all but disappeared; the glen became barren and desert-like, bounded by almost precipitous scree-covered slopes. The burn was now scarcely more than a trickle. As this landscape persisted for what seemed like miles, but may actually only have been one or two, Donald felt oppressed by a claustrophobic sense of enclosure, in effect of entrapment. Twice he attempted to climb up in the hope of gaining some sense of where he was, some lightening of the sense of pressure, but it proved impossible: he kept slipping back and was in danger of bringing a rush of rock hurtling down upon him. There was nothing for it but to keep plodding along the floor of the glen.

After what seemed an interminable interval the steep walls of the glen began to fall back and the track to move away from it onto a plateau of moorland. Now he could look back upon a magnificent vista and see the way by which he had ascended. The village miles below appeared cosy and welcoming, nestling in its wooded declivity, a wispy pall of smoke from numerous chimneys hanging above it; it gave no hint of the dark atmosphere of fraud and deceit which Donald had encountered there. He crossed the moorland, and now the path began to climb again into the foothills, behind which jagged and rocky mountains reared their heads.

At a place where the track was traversing a steep slope, with a particularly daunting decline on his left hand, the walker happened to kick a stone with the toe of his boot, and immediately loud and terrifying barking was heard from just around the coming bend. Donald was scared of large dogs at the best of times, and in his present particularly vulnerable situation the sound filled him with horror. There was no practicable way of making a detour, as a sheer rock-face bounded the path on the right-hand side, and if he did not brave this danger there would be no alternative but to turn back. Making use of the cover of a bush at the side of the track just on the bend, he peered cautiously around the corner.

Right against the cliff-face stood a ruined bothy, in front of which an enormous mastiff stood chained to a stake. Barking furiously and baring its teeth, it was hurling itself forward with such suicidal vehemence that it was almost surprising that it did not throttle itself or break its own neck. Its collar was furnished with sharp metal spikes; foam was at its lips. There was nothing for it but to pass the beast and trust that its chain would hold. For some reason Donald felt it impossible to compromise his dignity and run; but he certainly walked very fast indeed. The dog's efforts to burst free reached a crescendo and Donald believed he could hear a splitting noise from the stake. But all at once he was past, and only after he was out of sight round the next bend did he break into a run. Gradually the barking became less frenzied and eventually petered out in broken, baffled explosions of frustration and outrage.

The track was now heading up a *bealach*, a mountain pass which appeared as a distinct cleft in the rocky land-scape a couple of miles ahead. The traveller knew that once past this point he would look down into a differ-ent country. A feeling of excitement gripped him. The activity of walking, and his recent scare, kept him from brooding too much upon the fate of Madeleine and the schemes of the Sinister Cabaret, though a sense of determined purpose drove him forward unwearyingly. He had passed through a lightly wooded stretch and was not far from the summit when he heard a scrabbling of rocks to his right and a little behind him. When he turned to look he saw, aghast and unbelieving, a black bear descending the course of a dried-up burn. It flashed through his mind that environmentalists had been agitating for the return of extinct native species to the northern wilds, but surely things had not yet reached this stage! He wasn't sure whether the bear had seen him, and stood rooted to the spot in terror.

When it had reached the level of the track the bear stopped, looked up and saw Donald, clearly for the first time. It was about fifty yards away. He had no idea what was the right thing to do. The bear stood looking at him for a few very long moments, then snarled and stood up on its hind legs. Donald backed away slowly, and as he did so bent and picked up a stone in each hand. The bear dropped to all fours and loped forward unhurriedly. When it didn't stop, Donald hurled one stone and then the other: both fell short. The bear stopped for an instant, snarling, then moved forward again. Donald picked up another, heavier stone, steadied himself and threw it as hard as he could, aiming at the bear's head. This time, by great good fortune, it struck the animal squarely on the forehead, just above the left eye.

The animal gave a little howl, stopped, and raised a forepaw to the injured spot in an extraordinarily human fashion. A wave of sympathy passed through Donald

48

and he almost regretted his action. The bear suddenly reminded him of Wojtek (Voltek, as it was approximately pronounced), the Polish black bear which had arrived at Edinburgh Zoo with its sullen Polish keeper at the end of the war. Whenever his parents had taken him to the zoo Donald had insisted that the visit to Wojtek should be left till the last: 'Leaving the best bit to the end,' as with some tasty dish. 'I'm sorry, Wojtek,' he said now under his breath, quite carried away by the memory in spite of this situation of extreme danger. The beast hesitated, then, seeming to accept the apology, turned round quite suddenly and loped off down the path in the direction from which Donald had come.

This was getting to be a hazardous trip! But there was nothing to be done but press on, though now he kept a sharper lookout. About ten minutes after this incident he reached the summit of the pass, and saw below him a landscape of rocks, moorland and lochans. Ten miles away the horizon was broken by another range of hills: there was no sign of human habitation, nothing except the vapour trail of a jet to tell him that he was not on another planet.

When he had descended for about a mile the path forked and he had to consult his map. Unfortunately it proved of no help at all; while one of these tracks headed a little north-east, as he reckoned, and the other a little north-west, the map showed only one track crossing the moorland in a direction which he judged to run more or less between them. The alternative routes ran on opposite sides of a small loch, and he hazarded the guess that perhaps they would rejoin beyond it. Having nothing to guide him in his choice he spun a coin and took the right-hand path. After a mile it reached a T-junction; the other route must also join this further west, and he now inclined to the view that it was this that he should have taken.

But as he stood, still hesitating, he saw that the road – a much more substantial though still unsurfaced thorough-fare – led in the easterly direction to what looked like a substantial shooting-lodge. As it was no more than half a mile away he judged it sensible to make his way there to enquire which was the quickest route to Cul an Duirn. But he was by now very tired, and first he sat down on a rock to eat some lunch. Far away somewhere on his left he heard a shot. Stalking must be in progress: that meant there would certainly be someone at the lodge.

It was a long, rambling building of dark stone sur-rounded on three sides by thick woods. Smoke curled up from a chimney to the right of the front door. Three impos-ing stone steps led up to the entrance. Feeling scruffy and dirty, Donald rang the bell. In half a minute there appeared a handsome woman of about fifty, with striking red hair, streaked with grey, coiled about her head. They stared at each other for a moment or two with their mouths open, in equal and complementary astonishment. Good Lord! It was Moira Bannatyne! One of the great regrets of his repressed youth, and long married to his old pal Geoffrey, recently retired after a distinguished naval career!

Moira rushed forward, grabbed Donald by the hands and kissed him, not without feeling. 'Well, you're the sly one! Imagine not telling us you were coming – but you were always one for the unexpected! But how delight-ful – we were expecting you sometime, of course . . . ' she added, lest he should think her unwelcoming.

It was true, he now remembered. A vague invitation

had more than once been extended to him to pay a visit to Ben Despair Lodge, which Moira had inherited from an uncle a few years previously; but he had not been very serious about taking it up, and had no idea whatsoever that the place was anywhere in this vicinity. How very extraordinary! But he thought it best to go along with this understanding of his appearance: to explain how he had really come to arrive here was truly more than he could face.

'You see, I'd decided to do a bit of a walking tour in these parts, and I said to myself, "Well, why not call in on Geoff and Moira?" . . . but then I realized that I didn't have your number, so I thought I'd just saunter over the pass on the off-chance . . . '

It all sounded a bit lame, but Moira didn't seem to think anything of it.

'Great! Well, we've got a nice little party here just now. Sir Grossleigh Fatt – I don't think you'll know him. He's in bed snoring his head off at the moment, but the others are all out on the hill. There's Mrs Henn-Harrier . . . Maudie, you know? Yes, that's right; and then—'

(Here Donald thought he detected a slight cloud pass over Moira's enthusiastic features.)

'—Colonel Beaglehowl – Gerald. Quite a close friend of Geoff's. And ourselves; and now you! Come in and I'll show you to your room.' Moira took Donald's arm in hers and guided him through long dreary corridors and up eccentric stairs.

Up there, though, it was all very comfortable; Donald had a hot bath and then slept soundly for three hours. When he came down about six o' clock he felt ready for a drink. At the foot of the stairs Moira met him and grabbed hold of his hand.

'I'm glad you're here, Donald, I'm so worried! Mrs Henn-Harrier's still out on the hill. Geoff and Gerald walked back, of course, but Maudie was going to get a lift back on the bogie. Dougall told her to wait by the track while he went to load the stag onto the bogie with the help of our ghillie, Kevin Wagstaff. He's a former accounts manager with a surgical goods wholesaler in Staines, by the way. When they returned, there was no sign of her. Dougall thinks she may have taken the long way round by Deathtrap Corrie and the Breakneck Corridor. She's fanatical about exercise, you know.'

'I'm sure she'll be all right. She must know this country well?'

'Oh, yes! But Donald, you don't know the dangers of that route – in the darkness, with a wind getting up . . . '

'It's not dark yet.'

'But it's getting there . . . '

The three men were already drinking whisky in front of a roaring fire. The elegant Geoffrey was all *sang-froid*, accepting Donald's unexpected appearance quite nonchalantly. Sir Grossleigh Fatt was living up to his name, sitting deep in an armchair intent upon guzzling Pringle's Original Ridges and making little contribution to the conversation. As to Colonel Beaglehowl, he was as fine an English gentleman of the old school as could be encountered in a long day's march, and that was exactly what Donald had had, which made it all the more appropriate. He was clad, of course, in old but rather good tweeds, and had a high colour and a splendid reddish moustache flecked with distinguished grey. Close to his chair he had a lion-tamer's whip, which his huge but gentle Newfoundland dog eyed nervously from time to time.

They were discussing politics and Donald had remarkably little interest in what they had to say. None of the three seemed in the least concerned about the fate of Mrs Henn-Harrier; or perhaps they were merely feigning unconcern, intent upon projecting for the benefit of the weaker sex an image of unflappable realism and immunity to panic, born of long experience of tricky conditions and risks surmounted. They would bide their time until satisfied that the danger was real, one felt; but once so satisfied – ah, with what decision and competence and fearlessness they would act! Meanwhile, there was no call for unnecessary fuss. That sort of thing was only for old women of both sexes.

Poor Moira was aware of that, of course, but her concern for the safety of her missing guest would give her no peace, as Donald could easily tell.

Eventually she spoke up. 'It's after seven now, it's pitch black outside. What can have happened to Maudie?'

'Oh, I shouldn't worry about *her*,' said Beaglehowl. 'She's a tough old stick.'

Rather pointedly ignoring this judgement, Moira turned to her husband. 'What are we going to do, Geoffrey?'

'Eat, I should think.'

There was no answer to that. And eat they did, but it has to be conceded that it was a gloomy affair. There was no getting away from it now; the disappearance of Mrs Henn-Harrier was on everybody's mind. But generally speaking there was a tacit agreement that it would be in poor taste to refer to the matter. Geoffrey did so once, however, though with a certain studied obliquity.

'Wagstaff should have been keeping an eye on her, you know,' he remarked.

'Peasants!' cried Sir Grossleigh. 'How I wish the days would return when their lives were nasty, brutish and short.'

'I wouldn't go so far as that,' said Geoffrey.

'Kevin isn't *exactly* a peasant,' Moira put in. 'In fact he used to be an accounts manager with a surgical goods company in Staines.'

'Poh!' retorted Sir Grossleigh. 'Same thing.'

After that the meal proceeded uneventfully enough until the Colonel's gentle Newfoundland dared to raise his head a little from between his paws.

'Down, sir! Down!' Beaglehowl roared, his face apopleptic with rage, and cracked his whip with such extraordinary vehemence that he actually lassoed a wine glass and sent the contents, which happened to be red, cascading across the snow-white damask tablecloth.

'Oh, dear . . . sorry about that . . . ' How lame could an apology be?

'That's all right,' replied Moira without emphasis; but her face told a far different tale. Donald did not fail to observe a moment of dark bitterness casting its shadow across her features, a look such as is never elicited by the behaviour, however deplorable, of some casual acquaintance, but speaks of a lengthy and troubled history of stormy and confused passions which is not even yet at an end, and perhaps never will be. There are drumly undercurrents here, thought Donald. Oh, yes.

A coffee; a brandy; a cigar. Then Geoffrey said as casually as possible:

'Well, I think we should go and take a look.'

'I think I'll go to bed,' said Sir Grossleigh.

'Yes, Grossleigh, I think you should. You're too damn fat to be of any use to us on such an occasion as this. And Donald, this is no responsibility of yours. You've had a hard enough day already. Besides, too many cooks, and so on . . . Gerald and I will go. And Dougall.'

'Shall I bring my chanter?' asked the Colonel. 'It might give her heart . . . '

'No, a police whistle is better.'

'But I don't have one.'

'A police whistle is best.'

When they were gone Donald and Moira sat together on opposites sides of the dying fire. Donald was waiting for his old flame to bare something of her soul. Though neither spoke of it, they were both thinking of that quivering intensity of experience which they had always known in each other's company, in those long-gone days, thirty-five years ago or more, a current which had never found expression in word or deed but which now, it seemed for the first time, was tacitly but mutually acknowledged. When at last she spoke it was with a certain grandeur and pathos.

'There is something I have to tell you, Donald. Colonel Beaglehowl is not an Englishman. No, not a Scot either. It's much worse than that. The man with whom I have been having an affair for eight and a half years is in fact the Graf vom und zum Bagelhaul, son of one of Hitler's most trusted lieutenants. Laughable, isn't it? No, don't protest, the evidence is irrefutable. After the war he escaped with his family to the Argentine, and thence, eventually, to the United States, where he re-emerged in the sixties as Jerry Bagelhawl, an active and prominent member of the Student Non-Violent Co-ordinating Committee. That led on naturally to his becoming a stockbroker on Wall Street, but scandal was never far from his door and he had to flee once more. This time he ended up in England, where he insinuated himself into the best circles as Gerald Beaglehowl, Coldstream Guards, hero of Suez and former Master of the Cambridge University Drag. The rest is history.'

Donald was silent, reluctant to intrude upon a grief so recent and so raw.

'Listen to the bitter wind howling along the screes,' she continued after a charged silence, 'moaning through the branches of the dismal pines, seeking the very bone-marrow of the huddling hinds! Somewhere out there, in the lee of Ben Despair, Mrs Henn-Harrier is dragging her broken body. She is countless miles from habitation, racked with pain, in excruciating torment, the night is dark and dreadful, the ground sheer, rocky and inhospitable, her strength failing, she knows her efforts are in vain: yet the ungovernable spirit of survival will not let her rest. Drenched, freezing, mangled and lacerated, she yet hauls herself forward inch by inch, on her knuckles and one knee, dragging behind her her shattered and useless limb, praying to a God who will perhaps not save her. Help is at hand, is perhaps even now very near, but the night is impenetrably dark, the terrain daunting, the possibilities for the searchers incomputably innumerable, and she is too weak to cry out . . . Yes, somewhere out there Mrs Henn-Harrier is crawling towards an inexorable death; the man I have loved for ten years is an impostor . . . Donald, I'm so glad you are here with me tonight.'

5

The Sermon

It was very late when Donald, now safe and snug in his own bed, was aware of headlights partly softened by the curtains beaming briefly into his domain. Gravel crunched, car doors banged. The low voices of the returned search party were heard in muted, laconic exchanges, then Geoffrey said, 'Good night, Dougall'; and as the keeper's footsteps retreated towards his own quarters the massive front door closed and the iron bolt was driven home. Soon Ben Despair Lodge was silent as the grave in which, perhaps, Maudie Henn-Harrier would soon be laid.

Faces were sombre and words low and few as they helped themselves to the lavish grill temptingly arrayed on the hotplate the following morning. Only Sir Grossleigh appeared to have retained his appetite. A brooding restraint of complex origins paralysed Donald Humbie's will and prevented his asking the obvious questions, but the tears which Moira was obliged several times to dab at with her soaking handkerchief told their own depressing tale. The atmosphere of charged expectancy must eventually have reminded Geoffrey that Donald was still ignorant of what had befallen.

'She made it through Deathtrap Corrie,' he murmured half to himself, and almost as if it were a consolation. 'It was Breakneck Corridor that did for her.'

Donald half raised his chin and pursed his lips in acknowledgement, then dropped his eyes discreetly.

'What happened?' he inquired timidly.

'She broke her neck, of course! What else would happen in Breakneck Corridor?'

'True.'

'She was a game old gal,' said Sir Grossleigh.

Moira sobbed without shame.

'It's Sunday today,' observed Geoffrey a little redundantly. 'I think we should all go to church to pray for the soul of Maudie Henn-Harrier.'

It must be a Catholic church, thought Donald – or was Geoffrey simply ignorant of the nicer subtleties of Reformation theology? Probably the latter. The Pseudo-Beaglehowl was smirking a little into his coffee as if knew something that no-one else knew but was keeping it all to himself. Sir Grossleigh nodded solemnly and made one of those emphatic little grunts which people make during speeches when they want their assent to what has been said put, as it were, on record.

Moira left the room, clutching her handkerchief.

Donald let himself be carried along by the flow of events. They piled into a couple of four-wheel-drive vehicles and drove the five miles to the austere little church, associated with the obscure Dark Age Celtic saint, St Maelcontent. When the party of gentry sat down in their private pews a good deal of whispering broke out among the little congregation and continued intermittently throughout the service, especially during the prayers of intercession and even, and perhaps most of all, when they were praying for the friends and relations of Mrs Henn-Harrier – though not, as it indeed turned out, for her soul. Donald could make out some of the talk – it might even have been suspected that it was intended to be audible:

'That path up tae the kirk's a bloody disgrace. Speldering through glaur and cow shit every Sunday.'

'I know. All that's needed is a cattle grid.'

'Cattle grids cost money. Too damn mean.'

'Ay, right enough.'

And so on.

Donald had been led to expect that in his sermon the minister would without doubt dwell at some length on last night's tragedy. Mr Wotherspoon always made it topical, Moira said. But Donald had his doubts. The sermon had no doubt been written days before Mrs Henn-Harrier's death, and who really cared about that anyway? Why on earth would he go to the trouble of writing a new sermon? The minister was an earnest young man from the Central Belt who, according to Geoffrey, was 'a bit red', had some 'odd preoccupations' and wore a leather jacket on weekdays, but was generally acknowledged to preach a grand sermon. But as to that, let the reader judge.

'Not so long ago I was in the supermarket. (Better not say which one!) Standing in front of me in the check-out queue were a harassed mother and her small daughter.

The little girl was eyeing longingly the array of assorted sweets and other goodies so thoughtfully provided right at the check-outs by the supermarket management so that just such hungry tots as my little neighbour will wear down the resistance of their hard-put-upon parents and prevail upon them to BUY THE GOODS on display. The following conversation – or something very like it – now took place.

> *Little Girl*: Mummy, can I have some Smarties?
> *Mother*: No.
> *Little Girl*: Can I have some soor plums?
> *Mother*: No.
> *Little Girl*: Can I have some Hawick balls?
> *Mother*: No.
> *Little Girl*: Can I have some old-fashioned humbugs?
> *Mother*: No.
> *Little Girl*: Mummy, can I have some crisps?
> *Mother*: No.
> *Little Girl*: Can I have some Porky Scratchings?
> *Mother*: No.
> *Little Girl*: Mummy, why can I not have *anything* today?
> *Mother*: I didn't say you couldn't have *anything*, I only said you couldn't have *those* things. You can have a skelp on the bum for a start.

'And therewith she administered condign punishment. You see, friends, things do not always work out quite the way we expect. That little girl was expecting something nice but she ended up getting something really quite nasty, didn't she? People do things we don't expect; sometimes they're not really the people we think they are at all. And sometimes God, too, does things we don't expect, doesn't He? Who would have expected Him, for instance, to end so suddenly and so violently and so tragically the life of such a lovely person as Mrs Maudie Henn-Harrier? *So maybe God's not the person we think He is either.*

'That mother and her daughter were very much in my mind when, the other day, I pulled down from the shelf my old, well thumbed copy of the *Mystical Theology* of Pseudo-Dionysius. Pseudo-Dionysius was a monk who lived a very long time ago in a country called Syria, a sun-baked land near Lebanon, where, you may remember, people at one time used to go on holiday. We don't know his real name, but he wrote this book using the name of Dionysius the Areopagite, a man who is mentioned in the Acts of the Apostles as a convert of St Paul's.

'Nowadays authors are always quick to claim the credit for anything they write – if it's successful, of course! (Just imagine Irvine Welsh claiming that *Trainspotting* had been written by Dionysius the Areopagite!) But in olden days it was different. Then, it was the success of the book that mattered to the author, not his own fame and fortune, so if the author was unknown he might think, "Well, perhaps if I pretend this book was written by somebody famous people will want to read it and it will sell better." And that is just what this Syrian monk did: he called himself by the name of Paul's first convert, Dionysius the Areopagite.

'But one day someone came up to him and said, "See you, Dionysius, ca' yerself an Areopagite? Ye're juist a pseud."'

(The Pseudo-Beaglehowl stirred uneasily.)

'So his secret was out, and after that everyone called

him Pseudo-Dionysius, or Dionysius the (Pseudo-) Areopagite, or just plain Pseudo-Denys.

'That's a cracker, eh?

'Anyway, you may be wondering what all this has to
do with the little girl in the supermarket and her mother. I
don't blame you. But remember what I said earlier about
God maybe not being quite the person we thought He was.
And to explain what I mean by that, I don't think I can do
better than read you a passage – it's really quite a short
passage – from that well thumbed, and well loved, little
book of mine, the book by the Syrian monk from that
far-off time who called himself by the name of Dionysius
the Areopagite. He's talking about God. Here it is:

> It is not soul, or mind, or endowed with the faculty of
> imagination, conjecture, reason or understanding; nor is
> It any act of reason or understanding; nor can It be
> described by the reason or perceived by the understand-
> ing, since It is not number, or order, or greatness, or
> littleness, or equality, or inequality, and since It is not
> immovable or in motion, and has no power, and is not
> power or light, and does not live, and is not life; nor is
> It personal essence, or eternity, or time; nor can It be
> grasped by the understanding, since It is not knowledge
> or truth; nor is It kingship or wisdom; nor is It one, nor
> is It unity, nor is It Godhead or Goodness; nor is It
> Spirit, as we understand the term, since It is not Sonship
> or Fatherhood; nor is It any other thing such as we or
> any other being can have knowledge of; nor does It
> belong to the category of non-existence or to that of
> existence; nor do existent beings know It as It actually
> is, nor does It know them as they actually are; nor can

the reason attain to It to name It or to know It; nor is It darkness, nor is It light, or error, or truth; nor can any affirmation or negation apply to It; for while applying affirmations or negations to those orders of being that come next to It, we apply not unto It either affirmation or negation, inasmuch as It transcends all affirmation by being the perfect and unique Cause of all things, and transcends all negation by the pre-eminence of Its simple and absolute nature – free from every limitation and beyond them all.

'May God bless unto us this meditation on His Holy Word, and to His Name be glory and praise.'

Outside after the service, gathered doucely together in the stinking glaur, the congregation was loud in its praises of the homily.

'That was a grand sermon, eh?'

'Ay, the way he linked up the wee girl in the supermarket to that book – that was amazing.'

'You could never have seen that coming.'

'Nothing predictable from Rev. Wotherspoon. But he makes it all that clear.'

'I must be slow on the uptake, then,' remarked Donald ruefully to the last speaker. 'It was as clear as mud to me!'

'You just keep thinking about it, son,' replied the old woman, wagging a finger at the obtuse stranger, 'and one of these days the Lord will reveal His meaning!'

Donald was anxious to find out the way to Cul an Duirn, and at his behest Geoffrey, who had never heard of the place himself, started making enquiries of the locals, but they all shook their heads or shrugged their shoulders.

Eventually he came upon a very old man who knew what he was talking about. Donald was introduced to him so that he could take down directions, but he had no paper on him and asked the others of the party if any of them could oblige. Beaglehowl eagerly produced a bulging pocket-book and fumbled around in it until he managed to withdraw a dirty old piece of folded paper torn out of a notebook. When Donald opened it up he discovered, within, a grubby business card. He was about to return this to the Colonel when he noticed the name that was written on it. It read:

ALGERNON P. MOTION
Actor and Impersonator

Donald looked up in shock at Beaglehowl, who nodded back at him with that characteristic smirk of his which he now realized ought to have been instantly recognizable. Donald's heart sank.

Oh dear! Time to be off.

6

Pagan Country

Early that afternoon Donald was on the march again; not even the tears of Moira could detain him. Two business cards were in his pocket: that of the hateful impostor Motion, boastful of his ignominious calling; and that of the private detective MacNucator, whom the hard-pressed advocate now saw as his one hope and envisaged as the saviour who would return him to his dependable, familiar world and to the beloved wife, images of whose abduction, ignominy, abuse and even death haunted him waking and sleeping and drove him unrestingly on.

He had not dared to phone home from Ben Despair Lodge after his earlier experiences. The thought of confiding in Moira had crossed his mind, but the sheer oddity of what he would have had to relate had dissuaded him. It didn't fail to occur to him that she might even have doubted his sanity. The truth was that Donald was in a state of confusion and disorientation about everything that had happened to him since he had left home – what, three, four days before? Sometimes he felt that an immense gulf separated him from the whole of his past life, but at other times it seemed as if he had stepped out of it into the present minute only seconds before. It was rather like waking up from an anaesthetic: the moment of going under seemed remote, yet there was no sense of an intervening space of time.

The events at the guest house, the mad chase to the strange village, the Sinister Cabaret, the mountain walk and now even the interlude at Ben Despair Lodge felt shadowy and insubstantial. Yet when he set his mind to it he could remember every detail. At the moment he retained his sense of volition, but he knew that at any moment he might be returned to a state in which he was obliged almost passively to run with a train of happenings from which he felt he ought to be able to free himself by the exercise of his will, but in the event couldn't. This experience of powerlessness made him the more relentlessly set on the only goal which he was able to keep before his eyes – reaching Cul an Duirn and finding the detective.

Motion, that oily figure – who, or what, was he? Evil or laughable? To be feared or pitied? A danger or a mere nuisance? What was the meaning of his tricks? Their purpose? Was his malice general, or directed at Donald personally? If the latter, why? How did he manage the metamorphoses he effected? These questions scarcely differentiated themselves in Donald's troubled understanding. But he had a strong sense of the man's arrogant, barefaced effrontery, together with a half-formulated impression of a hollowness or vulnerability which underlay it and which held out a hope that he could be quite easily defeated, if only one knew how. There lay the rub.

He had entered the strath from the south-east and was now leaving it by a pass which headed north-west – in the direction of the sea, as he believed. The old man at the church had been vague about the distance but had said that it could easily be walked in a day. The sky was gloomy and overcast and the visibility poor, and a slight but persistent smirr of rain was slowly seeping through the walker's clothes. When he reached the head of the pass he looked down to a dim confusion of rock, heather and water merging into an impenetrable mist. The scene was almost unbearably barren, lonely and desolate. Donald almost wished he had never left Ben Despair Lodge or freed himself from Moira's despairing embrace. But there was no use looking back. There was nothing for it now but to press on.

He was approaching a small plantation of fir, where the steep defile gave on to more open ground, when he heard human squeals and howls interspersed with a dull thwacking sound. Hurrying on, though in some trepidation, he saw, in front of a substantial log hut with a corrugated iron roof deep among the trees, an enormous beefy individual in the brown habit of a Capuchin friar belabouring with a leather belt a grotesquely overgrown schoolboy, reminiscent of Billy Bunter played by an adult actor, wearing a school cap and a black leather suit with shorts and mounted on a rearing horse. This character seemed the identical twin of the friar who was beating him.

Donald's astonishment was considerable: this was not, after all, the kind of scene one expects to encounter in a remote glen in north-west Scotland in early October. The friar rained blows on the fat schoolboy indiscriminately from every angle, many of which, sadly, landed on the unfortunate horse – which whinnied pitifully and tried to bolt. The friar grabbed hold of the reins and bellowed: 'Get off that fucking horse!' continuing to lay on with the belt while his victim shielded himself as best he could.

As Donald watched open-mouthed, another, much older friar, thin and ascetic, appeared at the door of the hut and leaned against the doorpost smiling slightly to himself and nodding in apparent approval. After a minute or so the schoolboy fell off the horse and ran off puffing and yelling 'Yaroooh!' – with the irate friar in hot pursuit, still letting fly with his leather belt. The horse meanwhile slumped to the ground on its haunches and commenced rubbing its injured neck with its right foreleg in a touching and most human gesture.

Donald turned towards the older friar in utter outrage.

'What the devil is going on here?' he cried. 'What a disgraceful scene!'

'Oh, you must forgive Brother Intolerans,' the other replied evenly. 'You see, he is a thin man at heart. That other person is the fat man inside him, whom he has to get rid of once and for all if he is to be successful in the ascetic life. The fat man wants to stay where he is, of course – he is quite content there. So, unfortunately, Brother Intolerans is having to resort to violent means to evict him.'

'Well, I dare say . . . ' said Donald, somewhat non-plussed, 'but why should the poor horse have to suffer? Didn't you see how it was catching half the blows?'

'Yes, it's unfortunate, but I'm afraid that's just the way

things are.' The friar made this observation with some complacency, and seemed secretly even to take a certain satisfaction from what he said.

'Well, I think it's bloody awful. Excuse my language, Father, but I find this quite upsetting.'

'Please call me Brother – I am in fact a priest, but in our order we are all addressed as Brother. – Would you care to honour our humble abode by coming in for a cup of tea and a jeely piece? You'd be welcome to stay the night – you're a long way from habitation.'

'Thank you, but I think I'd choke after what I've just witnessed. Besides, I've got a lot more ground to cover before nightfall.'

'Up to yourself. But I must warn you that you will soon be entering pagan country. You may encounter worse there.'

'Thanks, I'll take my chance.'

'As you will. Peace be with you.'

Just out of thrawnness, and in spite of being ravenously hungry, Donald walked for another mile or so before eating the sandwiches which Moira had lovingly prepared for him with her very own hand, but as he huddled against a rock in the bone-numbing damp, mist billowing about his ears, he didn't fail to regret the warm retreat of the morally questionable Capuchins. All the same, the sun was showing signs of being about to struggle through; and as he continued his descent Donald gradually came into a less desolate and barren landscape, a gentler country with deciduous trees scattered here and there which slowly became more plentiful until he was walking through a rich woodland made bright by plentiful berries of rowan and hip and by a rich carpet of fungi which formed a variegated pattern on the forest floor.

The weak but now clearly visible sun was rapidly declining when the traveller stepped out of the wood on to a platform of open ground standing above a steep descent towards the coast and a maze of tangled promontories. The sea lay before him, calm, grey and with a deathly chill upon it. He paused for a moment, but was about to stride on when he heard from over on his right a low, eerie chanting. Where the little plateau abutted on a rocky height there stood a circular altar or pyre built of rough stonework on which a wood fire burned lustily. A few people were kneeling around it and a group of perhaps a dozen more stood watching at a short distance. Donald retreated a little way into the wood then crept to his right in the direction of the pyre until he reached the nearest point at which he felt he could watch safely and unobserved.

The fire consisted of a number of stout logs roughly arranged in a rudimentary tent shape. In the hollow thus formed lay what at first he took to be another log, but as he gazed Donald saw with horror that it appeared to be moving, as if it were something living which was endeavouring vainly to rise. Though he could not see clearly from his still rather distant vantage point, it seemed to him to resemble the head and neck of a horse. Suddenly a man who had been kneeling stood up, went over to the pyre and started prodding at the moving thing with a short stick. At this there arose some cries of seeming outrage from the bystanders – whom Donald now sensed were hostile to what was taking place – and several of them rushed forward and started beating the man.

For a minute or two there was confused fighting and

cries of rage and pain, then the man broke loose and ran off and disappeared down the slope. But the fury of the disaffected group, who considerably outnumbered the worshippers, had not been appeased. Someone shouted something about 'Hezekiah', and pointed, and now they took hold of another kneeling figure with angry cries, crowding round him and slapping him on the face. This was a thin, dirty, malicious-looking old man with white stubble on his face. He showed no fear or sign of repentance but snarled defiantly at his captors. One of them now came forward with a rope; this was secured round the old man's ankles and they hoisted him up and hung him upside down from the branch of a tree and commenced beating him with sticks. The malicious old man twisted and flailed and spat venom at his tormentors.

The old friar had been right – this was pagan country indeed! Crouching low, Donald turned and weaved his way back through the trees by the way he had come. When he reached the track he crossed it and continued through the wood for some way on the other side before cautiously emerging, traversing the open ground (the gathering at the pyre now quite far off but still thronged around the tree from which Hezekiah was hung), and descending the slope. He was considerably shaken by what he had witnessed, but this strange journey had begun to inure him to odd sights and experiences, and once they were behind him he found it strangely easy to shrug his shoulders and dismiss them from his mind. Besides, he had to concentrate on reaching his goal: if he did not make Cul an Duirn within the next hour or so he was in danger of being benighted.

At last the path descended almost to the level of the

shore and joined a single-track paved road. Not far along the road to the north he could see the low whitewashed buildings of a substantial settlement which proved indeed to be Cul an Duirn. After a couple of hundred yards he found himself at the door of a scruffy, run-down hotel. The whitewash was flaking off the walls, the window frames were rotting, and empty beer kegs stood amongst litter outside the bar door. It all looked dreary and lifeless, but Donald was so tired that he didn't care. The receptionist greeted him with an almost hostile indifference, but at least there was a room available, cold and depressing though it was. After eating a bowl of tinned soup and a cellophane-wrapped sandwich in the bar, he bathed in a bathroom probably undecorated since the forties, and, dead tired and his brain incapable of taking further stock of his situation, went straight to bed and plunged at once into the depths of a dreamless sleep.

After breakfast the following morning, feeling refreshed and almost optimistic, Donald went down the road to the Spar shop for his morning paper. He was considering, in fact, what friendly small talk would serve to introduce his intended enquiry about the detective. But the shopkeeper, a small unsmiling elderly man in glasses, inspected him briefly and with apparent distaste, then announced without explanation:

'I'm not serving you.'

Donald's mouth dropped open. 'Why?'

'Because I know who you are. You've just escaped from prison.'

'You're a fool,' replied Donald, coldly and with great self-possession. 'You may well have seen me leaving the prison but I was no doubt there in furtherance of my professional duties. I am an advocate, a Queen's Counsel. Think before you speak, next time, if you are capable of it.' And then he was quite unexpectedly seized with a cold fury and directed a volley of abuse at the shopkeeper, calling him every insulting name that came into his head, until the man, unable to stand up to the onslaught any longer, went and lay down in a small recess or alcove opposite the till and curled up there in a foetal position, his thumb in his mouth, apparently comatose or even dead.

'Oh, you faker!' Donald shouted at him. 'Stop carrying on like that! Get up and do your bloody job!' He slammed the money for his paper on the counter and walked out. He had that curious feeling of disorientation again, as if things were apparently normal and yet not quite as they should be. The little man in the shop had behaved somewhat irrationally, it couldn't be denied. Yet perhaps Donald had over-reacted. Yes, that's what it was: he kept over-reacting. It was such a useful concept in times of trouble.

But worse trouble was to come. When Donald got back to his room at the hotel he opened the door to find it occupied by three people! – a seedy-looking couple in their thirties and a little girl of two or three who stood sucking her thumb and staring at him with blank eyes. A camp bed had been moved in for her. The couple gazed at him indifferently as he stood there open-mouthed.

'What's going on?' he gasped. 'This is *my* room!'

'This is where they put us,' said the man with a shrug.

'But they can't do this without consulting me! I said I was staying for two or three nights . . . ' Donald was boiling with fury but aware that it wasn't the couple's fault, which made him the more frustrated and enraged.

'Seems they overbooked,' said the man, shrugging once more.

'But my things! What have they done with my things?'

'Oh, ay,' said the woman, and pulled Donald's backpack from under the bed.

It had not been properly fastened, and all Donald's possessions had simply been crammed in any-old-how, with contemptuous indifference. He was about to protest once more, but, seeing their stupid faces, he realized that there was nothing to be looked for from that quarter, and instead charged off downstairs with his baggage to confront the management.

Behind the desk was a man he had not seen before but who yet had a disquieteningly familiar look about him. He was in his shirt sleeves and wore a joke tie featuring a jolly-looking fish standing on its tail, in top hat and bow tie and carrying a swagger-stick under its fin. The man's hair was fair and the face was a bit altered, but Donald was convinced he knew who it was . . .

'How can I help you, sir?' enquired the manager equably.

'What the hell's going on here? I've been turfed out of my room—'

'I'll be with you in a few moments,' he said, and turned away to some papers on the desk, concentrating on them with odious affectation.

'Make it quick, please!' cried Donald. 'I haven't all day!'

Just as the fellow seemed about to attend to Donald, the man from the bedroom appeared at the latter's shoulder and the manager immediately transferred his attention to the newcomer.

'Could we have a potty for the wee girl?' the man asked.

'Of course, of course, Mr Reilly! I'll see to it right away, sir!' And he shot off without so much as a glance at Donald. Such was the advocate's fury that when the manager reappeared after at least five minutes he grabbed him by the tie and pulled him towards him across the desk.

The creature merely smiled.

'Don't think I can't see through you, you wretched impersonator!' Donald cried. 'I know who you are: we've met before! At Fliuchary, then again at Ben Despair Lodge. You're Motion, you swine, you're the leader of the Sinister Cabaret! What have you done with my wife?'

'Case of mistaken identity, I'm afraid,' replied the other with great equanimity, freeing himself gently but firmly from Donald's now faltering grasp. 'My name's Hotchkiss. I came here from Morecambe three years ago. – Now then, we've had to rearrange the rooms. You're in the Cell of St Lawrence, but I can't let you in until the paperwork is completed . . . Just coming, Murdo,' he responded to a call from the bar, and went off again, leaving Donald standing stupidly once more.

But Donald *wasn't* standing for it, and followed him through.

'Look here,' he shouted, 'I want into my room now!'

'One moment, please – the files are in the truck.' Hotchkiss was standing beside the open hatch into the cellar, and Donald was seized by an impulse to dart round the bar and hurl the manager down the hatch. But the man seemed to read his thoughts instantly, and looked at Donald and then down at the hatch, and then back at Donald once more, smiling sardonically.

'The files are in the truck,' he repeated, and walked through the bar and out into the yard. A filthy old van stood there with the engine running – a man was in the driving seat. Donald could actually see a couple of dirty pink folders on the back seat; but even as the manager walked lazily in the direction of the van the driver revved the engine and drove off. Hotchkiss turned to Donald and raised his hands in mock despair, grinning insolently.

Balked – thwarted – dispossessed! Why was this happening to him? Donald had had enough. Shouldering his backpack, he turned away with a snarl of rage and contempt and strode off through the yard to the road.

'I won't charge you for last night!' Hotchkiss called after him.

And there was no mistaking that mocking laugh.

7

The Mountain Dew

Midday found Donald settled at a table in a pub called the
Mountain Dew with a steak pie and a pint. He wanted
to get the feel of the place before making his enquiries
about the detective. Opening the local paper, he was a
little astonished to find that the main story was of the
accidental death of Mrs Henn-Harrier. He had not dreamt
it all, then. In fact, the leading article was devoted to the
philosophical implications of that sad event.

'This morning,' he read, 'decent, ordinary people across
the land will be asking themselves: Why did God not save
Mrs Henn-Harrier? Can we imagine a loving God who
wouldn't *want* to save such a lovely lady? It is a question
which brings us up short. For some of us, the bottom line
will now always be this: not "Does God exist?" – none
of us knows that – but, if He does exist and yet failed to
save Mrs Henn-Harrier, do we want to have anything to
do with Him? After all, would we want to rub shoulders

with a murderer? Someone who had gunned down in the street, without provocation, such a lovely person as, let's say, Mrs Henn-Harrier? No, most of us wouldn't. So why should it be any different with God? This is supposed to be an omnipotent God! A God of love! So what about Mrs Henn-Harrier? Eh? We think we should be told.'

Aw, cummon, thought Donald. I mean, when is He to intervene and when isn't He? If only selectively, it's not really fair, is it? But if always, then we are reduced to automata. He felt quite pleased with this formulation. Well, that's that little metaphysical quandary dealt with, he concluded, looking around him with ill-humour.

They seemed to be an odd lot of people in Cul an Duirn, and Donald noted that they spoke in a wide variety of accents. He wondered just where exactly the place could be. Was this really the West Highlands? Wasn't it rather Caithness, perhaps, or even Moldavia? Although it was quite early in the day many of the customers in the Mountain Dew were already noticeably drunk, and getting drunker rapidly. A man straight out of the 1950s, wearing an ancient double-breasted bottle-green suit with trousers that were far too long for him, and with greasy black hair in the Tony Curtis or Duck's Arse style, emerged from a snug carrying a nearly full pint glass, staggered a few steps, and then fell flat on his face.

No-one paid the slightest attention.

The man picked himself up and staggered back to the snug. Eventually the barman, sighing and shaking his head, came over with a dust pan and swept up the broken glass, spreading the spilt beer more evenly across the floor.

Then another very drunk man started playing a game

with a five-pound note: with immense concentration, he repeatedly held the note a couple of feet above a chair, let it drop, then slammed the flat of his hand down upon it just as it landed. When he had performed this diverting trick perhaps a dozen times the barman, with a look of resignation, walked calmly over to him, grabbed him by the collar and lifted him first to and then right off his feet, and manhandled him out the door. All this was evidently just in the day's work, and it was far from over. A few minutes later a man who was clearly significantly less than the full shilling came in with a drunken old harridan, apparently his mother. No sooner had they sat down at a table than the barman strode over to them, picked the man with learning difficulties up by the tie and the belt, carried him out through the door and dropped him on the pavement, while the old woman screamed ineffectual obscenities. All in the day's work. And it was only twenty past twelve in the afternoon.

Donald must have looked surprised, for the barman volunteered the explanation:

'He's barred.'

'Ah!' replied Donald. Put like that, it indeed seemed perfectly reasonable.

The visitor began to find himself the object of local curiosity. It had taken a little time to register that there was someone unfamiliar in the bar, but once that had happened Donald found himself surrounded by red, bulbous faces staring at him open-mouthed out of rheumy, bloodshot eyes; faces which might have escaped from a Flemish painting. They pointed, then started making odd spluttering noises, as if they were attempting to speak but not finding it easy.

'Frensh?' said one, his face just an inch or two from Donald's.

'French? No, I'm Scottish as a matter of fact.'

But the idea was hard to shift.

'You Frensh?' asked another, then repeated it:

'*Frensh?*' As if Donald were deaf, foreign, stupid or all three, but certainly incapable of understanding even one single word without assistance.

The bulbous faces began to swim before his eyes.

But now a saviour appeared. A stolid Slavonic visage was advanced through the jostling throng and the huge, weathered hand of a peasant was held out for him to grasp.

'Allow me, sir. I am Arkady Vasilyevich Pachydermatov. Please excuse my friends. They are rough, but harmless. They will not hurt you.'

And indeed they all began at once to melt away.

Donald was so impressed that he asked Arkady what he was drinking.

'Ah, thank you, sir. I will have a double vodka . . . I came here as a Klondiker, you see, seeking the gold in your Scottish seas, but the Mountain Dew held me fast and I have never yet succeeded to return home to my beloved Russia or to Anastasia Ignatyevna who awaits me still, sir, waits for me with tears that will never cease to well up in her throat until the day of my return. I refer to my wife, sir, my little Pachydermatova. It sounds like a very terrible skin disease, I know, but blame the holy patron of our family, from whom we derive our name, St Pachyderm of Shchdroulkhov (1739–1821), a Holy Fool if ever there was one, who sat submerged up to his waist in a bucket of frozen water every year from Advent until

Pentecost, praising God without ceasing. And you know, sir, that our Russian winters are harsh. He never moved from the bucket for any purpose whatever and his food was brought to him daily by a friendly Harper's snow bunting.'

'And in the warmer months?'

'From Pentecost until Advent the blessed Pachyderm was submerged up to the waist in a vat of boiling *shchi*, our Russian cabbage soup.'

'Praising God the while?'

'Ceaselessly.'

'And why do you not return home, Arkady Vasilyevich?'

'Ah, good sir, do not torment me! Because I am weak, sir, weak and a worm! Trample upon me, grind me under your heel until I am in two parts: one part, the better, will attempt to crawl back to Mother Russia, to Anastasia Ignatyevna and to my little Sofia Arkadyevna who was the joy of my life; but the worse half – and that the larger – will infallibly and resolutely creep right back in here, sir, right back into the Mountain Dew! Oh, I am vile, sir, *vile!*' Arkady Vasilyevich buried his head in his big hands and began to sob inconsolably:

'Oh, if only my little Sofia Arkadyevna were here she would save me! How meekly she would stand outside the door of this house of sin and shame, sir, in her rags and tattered shawl, waiting for me, willing me to come home! How meekly, sir, and how long! "Away down tae the Mountain Dew, Sofia Arkadyevna," Anastasia Ignatyevna would say to her, "an' get that faither o' yours oot o' there an' hame tae his tea afore his tatties a' turn tae mush." And I would come, sir! Oh, how meekly and with what joy I would come!' And he burst into another fit of pitiable sobbing.

'Have another vodka, Arkady Vasilyevich. Then you'll feel better. By the way, my name's Donald – Domhnall Ruadh Phadraig Fhionnlaigh, as a matter of fact, though some people call me Hippo. God knows why – I look nothing like a hippopotamus, do I? The largest living non-ruminating even-toed mammal?'

'No, but that is life, sir,' said Arkady Vasilyevich, nodding sagely and looking, in fact, quite reconciled to life as he downed his umpteenth vodka.

'No today naebody calls you Hippo,' interrupted the barman quite aggressively. 'This is the Dark Night of the Patronymics. Everybody gets called proper. An' the Dark Night starts at midday. See, most of the year I'm Kenny Squeezebox, but no today. Today I'm Coinneach Eachainn Uilleim an Clarsair Odhar. Same for everybody. Only exception is Big Hieronymus there. He's a Dutchman, and the Dutch don't have patronymics. He mostly gets called Geronimo, but there's a few cry him Jerome. He disnae like Jerry.'

Hieronymus was the leering grotesque who had accused Donald of being Frensh.

'What are you drinking, Ingibjorg Sigurdsdottir, my beauty?' enquired Arkady Vasilyevich Pachydermatov drunkenly, attempting to put his arm around the waist of a large-boned and high-cheekboned blonde who had just made her way up to the bar.

He was summarily repulsed:

'Nothing at all from you, Arkady Vasilyevich!'

'Let me!' cried Donald much too eagerly. 'Will it be a schnapps, perhaps?' he added with an arch gallantry.

'No. A Bacardi and coke, thank you, a Dhomnaill Ruadh Phadraig Fhionnlaigh.'

'Well remembered, Ingibjorg Sigurdsdottir!'

The flirtatious badinage, thus initiated, continued divertingly enough for some time. But all the while there was a distracting niggle at the back of Donald's mind. He was already getting drunk, of course, but even with one arm across the shoulders of Arkady Vasilyevich and the other around the waist of Ingibjorg Sigurdsdottir he was still sober enough to remember the real reason for his presence in the Mountain Dew. He was there to find out about the detective. He had to keep that purpose clearly before his eyes or he would soon be washed away in a swill of alcohol and unreality, but it was deeply lodged in a place at the bottom of his mind which it was becoming ever harder to reach. But then he happened to glance in the direction of a board to the side of the bar to which were pinned notices advertising coming events – folk nights, dances, community council meetings and so on. One of them hit him right between the eyes:

THE SINISTER CABARET
COMING SOON

Donald's heart leapt into his mouth! He was instantly sober – or at least sober enough. He leaned towards the barman.

'Tell me, a Choinnich Eachainn Uilleim an Clarsair Odhar, do you happen to know a detective hereabouts by the name of Peter MacNucator?'

'You mean Peadar Sheumais Iain?'

'That'll be him.'

By way of answer the barman nodded over Donald's right shoulder, and he turned to see a small, wiry man with grey hair, in a black seaman's jersey, whom he had noticed earlier sitting by himself at a table by the wall, occasionally sipping a malt whisky and observing the goings-on around him with a penetrating and ironic look in his eye and a satirical but not unkindly smile about his lips.

'You'll be looking for me?' Peter MacNucator asked.

The Detective

8

Anamnesis

'Tell me, Peter, is there much work for a detective round here? Okay, I dare say there are a few riots in the Mountain Dew on a Friday night, but there won't be a lot of detection involved in sorting that out, eh?'

The little detective laughed. They had gone back to his cottage on the road north out of the village and were settled in front of a peat fire with a bottle of Lagavoulin on the table between them.

'You're not far out about the riots, right enough. Two months ago we had a wedding reception in the Mountain Dew. Rather an unusual wedding, because it was a MacPhee marrying a Williamson, which isn't far off a Montague marrying a Capulet. Tinker clans, you know. Enemies since before the Flood. Well, it started off amicably enough, but of course it didn't last. Five minutes in the Mountain Dew and they were breaking chairs over each other's heads. But Kenny Squeezebox sorted them out no bother. The polis weren't called. But to answer your question:

'To tell the truth I'm semi-retired, but I come out of hibernation when someone needs me. I was in the polis myself at one time, took early retirement and came back home. But you'd be surprised at the number of people who come knocking at my door with their little problems. Come from all over, actually. Where did you hear about me yourself?'

'Oh, it was a Mr Chisholm who gave me your card. Mr Chisholm in the hardware store in . . . it's over that way, somewhere . . . ,' said Donald lamely, embarrassed that he had no idea of the name of the place where the Sinister Cabaret had performed that night.

'Ay, I think I know where you mean,' said MacNucator, smiling to himself enigmatically. 'So, Mr Humbie – or would you prefer me to call you Donald? – Good. So, what exactly is the nature of your problem, Donald?' He crossed his legs, rested his elbow on his knee and his chin in his hand, and, leaning forward, gazed intently at his client.

Donald realized that it was going to be no easy matter to explain just what the nature of his problem was. 'Well . . . Did you happen to notice that poster back in the pub advertising an act called the Sinister Cabaret? Yes. Well, it's all to do with them. That set of impostors. But how did I get involved with them – or what have they got to do with me? That's much harder to say. Much harder. Do you know anything about them yourself, er . . . Peter?' He wanted to put off recounting his humiliating and belief-challenging story.

'I know enough, but none of it will be of any use until

I've heard your story.'

Donald took a sip, almost a gulp if the truth be known, of Lagavoulin to steady his nerves. 'True. Right then. Last week – less than a week ago, actually, though it seems like a lifetime – I went off on holiday. By myself, without my wife. I'm a QC, by the way, I live in Edinburgh.'

MacNucator nodded as if he knew this already.

'The truth is, I've not been so well lately. I needed to get off by myself for a bit, be alone, you know? Don't get me wrong: no domestic problems, I love my wife, she loves me, but . . . Well, it was Madeleine who suggested it, actually. We all need space sometimes, don't we? Yes . . . '

He was drifting.

MacNucator kept staring at him fixedly though, not moving or changing his expression. Not so much all ears as all eyes.

'So, to cut a long story short. I arrived at the guest house in Fliuchary where Madeleine and I have been going for years. Mrs Macrae's. She's a delightful old lady – well, not that old really . . . ' He felt himself shuddering. 'Or was. She wasn't there. Instead, there was this oily bastard who called himself Motion – the leader of this wretched "Cabaret", as it turned out. He'd usurped everything. The house: it was all the same, down to the very last detail, nothing changed; except that Mrs Macrae had gone, and he was there instead. She was dead, so he claimed. If she is, then I think he killed her.' Donald felt a racking sob pass through him; it surged up through his chest but somehow stuck in his throat then emerged, transformed, as a snarl of fury.

'Go on,' said the detective, when he had recovered.

Donald sighed bitterly. 'I've missed out something really quite grotesque. I suppose I'm a bit worried that you'll think me crazy. Anyway. The previous night I'd phoned home, from Benderloch. To tell the truth, I was going to suggest that Madeleine join me after all – I was feeling lonely. The answering machine was on. That was odd enough in itself, because Madeleine never goes out alone – or scarcely ever. But some depraved practical joker seemed to have got at the machine, claiming to be . . . Attila the Hun . . . ' Donald, who had been looking at his hands while he spoke, now glanced over at MacNucator in embarrassment.

But the detective was not laughing.

'In retrospect, I'm certain the voice was Motion's.'

'Gets around a bit, doesn't he?' The tone was not really ironic.

'So it would appear. I would have got out then and there, but when the phone had failed to . . . work, I'd e-mailed Madeleine with the message to join me, and though there had been no reply I still hoped she might turn up. So I stayed overnight. A terrible night I had – appalling nightmares.'

'Did they have anything to do with Motion?' asked the detective at once, to Donald's surprise.

'Oh, yes, they did in fact – and his wife too. I forgot to mention his wife. I hadn't seen her in the flesh at that point – just her photograph.'

And with some reluctance he told MacNucator about his lascivious dreams in which Madeleine and Mrs Motion had kept interchanging their shapes, and of Motion's pimping part.

The detective listened without comment but with keen

attention, clearly taking everything in.

'The next morning I tried the phone again. Same voice. Motion's. But this time it simply said that the house was no longer mine! How do you like that? Not very encouraging, was it? And still nothing from Madeleine. But that afternoon, when I got back to the guest house after a walk, Motion met me and told me that my wife had arrived and was upstairs sleeping. So up I went, all excited, and sure enough there she was lying in bed. Or so it appeared.'

So far Donald had managed to remain reasonably calm and in control of himself, but at this point the horror of his experience overwhelmed him and he burst into hysterical laughter which all the same had something forced about it; he half realized himself that he was indulging the hysteria in order to put off describing what it was necessary to describe.

The detective was probably aware of this too, and waited impassively for the attack to subside.

'The hair was real enough,' Donald managed to articulate at last, wiping his tears away, 'but that was all that was. Madeleine's hair, glued onto the head of a rag-doll. Can you imagine it? A life-size rag-doll! What sort of a person would think up something like that?'

'That's a very good question. And how did you react?'

'I fled. Couldn't take any more. I just leapt into the car and drove off – took the first turning off the main road I could find. They were following me, you see – the Motions. For a bit, at least. But I must have eluded them.'

Donald told the detective of his experiences in the deserted hotel in the unnamed village, of the deaf mutes and of the bizarre performance by the Sinister Cabaret.

MacNucator seemed strangely unsurprised by what he heard, though he took it all very seriously, only now and again permitting himself a restrained, almost private smile. He gave the impression of thinking hard as he listened, and occasionally asked his client to expand on something. It was as if he already had a theory in mind.

'When Madeleine appeared on the stage with them – or seemed to – what did you feel about that?'

'What did I *feel*? Outrage, of course! They had stolen my wife, done away with her – taken her from me!' Donald started sobbing. It was disgraceful, but he absolutely couldn't help himself.

'You were quite sure, were you, that it wasn't her on the stage? Certain that she wasn't in it with them?'

'What a suggestion! But of course I'm sure! My wife conspire against me with those vulgarians? Madeleine loves me, I told you that! Besides, I know my own wife when I see her. It was like her, I grant you, *very* like her, virtually identical – but just a simulacrum, all the same! Just a substitute, provided by that impostor! Just as much as that rag-doll was. Madeleine with the heart plucked out of her! That's what they're all about, isn't it, this Sinister Cabaret? Pretence, imposture, impersonation, usurpation?'

'That's certainly true, right enough,' said the imperturbable detective. 'But you say you confronted them afterwards?'

'Yes, by all means I confronted the bastards. Demanded to know what they had done to my wife!'

'And?'

'They just laughed. Claimed she was one of them now. One of them actually had the cheek to say, "What have *we* done to her? What have *you* done to her, don't you mean?"'

'Hmm – interesting. What do you think was meant by that?'

'Search me! How should I know?'

MacNucator was silent for a few moments, thinking, staring out of the window at the rapidly darkening sea. Then he asked:

'You said you thought you remembered one or two of them from the past?'

'Yes! That swine Cant. Cant, the school bully. Haven't seen him for forty-five years, but I'm certain it was him. It would be in character, all right. He seemed to be the hotel owner – Cant's Hotel. Then there was another of his gang – we used to call him Scrote.'

'Do you think Cant is the connection? I mean, you'd never seen the others before? What would they have to do with you?'

'Well, how can you tell with impostors like that? They might be impersonating anybody.'

'That is quite true. So. You decided not to contact the police. Mr Chisholm recommended me instead? That was kind of him. Wise, too. And you told me that you walked here. Tell me about your journey.'

'It wasn't uneventful. First of all, right in the middle of nowhere, up in the high moorland, a great mastiff tied to a stake tried to attack me. I thought it was going to break free, but thank God, it didn't succeed. Then – you won't believe this, but it's true – a black bear came at me down a gully! I drove it off with stones – actually I think I may have hurt the poor brute. I rather hope not.'

'You overcame some hazards, right enough. But the Cabaret: no sign of them?'

'Oh, yes, they caught up with me – or at least Motion did. At Ben Despair Lodge.' And Donald went on to tell the detective about Colonel Beaglehowl, the last hours of Mrs Henn-Harrier, and of how he had come into possession of Motion's business card.

'So what you're saying', said the detective, rubbing his chin thoughtfully, 'is that Beaglehowl not only wasn't Beaglehowl, or Jerry Bagelhawl, but he wasn't the Graf vom und zum Bagelhaul either – in spite of what your friend Moira called "irrefutable evidence"?'

'No, he was Motion, I'm certain of it – the master impersonator. And he *meant* me to find his card. That's why he was there, of course. He must have pursued me there somehow.'

'But you say your friend claimed to have been having an affair with him for – what? – eight and a half years? With Beaglehowl, that is? So he can't have been at Ben Despair Lodge just because of you, can he?'

Donald felt oddly offended at this and threw up his hands in exasperation:

'You're the detective – you tell me! Perhaps he was impersonating Beaglehowl, or Bagelhaul, or whatever. Just on this occasion. Perhaps there's also a real Beaglehowl, or a real Bagelhaul. How should I know? How do you expect me to find my way about this hateful hall of mirrors?' He was just about to say, 'That's what I'm paying you for,' but fortunately he desisted.

'Hmm. And after you left the lodge – anything special happen on your way here?'

Donald related the extraordinary happenings of the friar

beating his replica, the fat schoolboy on the horse, the sacrificial altar and the burning log which became the head of a horse, and the lynching of the malicious old man. As usual MacNucator listened intently, but his only comment was:

'A bad day for horses.'

'Oh, a terrible day for horses,' Donald agreed, and quite inexplicably he began to cry.

'You're tired,' the detective said kindly. 'We'll have something to eat then we'll go to bed. And we'll talk more about all of this tomorrow.'

In the morning Donald looked out of the window in the little cabin-like bedroom at the back of MacNucator's cottage – where he was installed, by the detective's generosity, for as long as he wanted to stay – and decided that he would like to see a doctor. He felt, not for the first time since he had left home, that there was something not quite right in his head. As he gazed at the shifting mist which wrapped the mountains to the east, out of which he had walked the previous day, he experienced a sense of mysterious otherness which he could neither analyse nor account for, but he felt that in some obscure way it lay not in what was before his eyes but within himself.

It was like a physical illness, though not in all respects an unpleasant one. He had the impression, too, that what he was experiencing had something to do with Motion and the Sinister Cabaret, but whether as cause or effect, or as something less straightforward than either, he couldn't make out. Was he ill? Before he went further with the detective he wanted to be clear about that. It wasn't that he thought he was going crazy; but perhaps he was concerned that Peter would think he was.

MacNucator shook his head and smiled a little ambiguously. 'Go and see Dr Conradi by all means,' he said. 'Anything that will help to set your mind at ease can only help me. Oh, yes.'

There was no shining new Health Centre in Cul an Duirn. As used to be the way in remote Highland places, the doctor held a surgery a couple of days a week in the front room of a private house, and by good fortune this happened to be one of those mornings.

Dr Conradi proved to be a bald, angular man with a black patch over one eye and a cold, appraising look in the other. Donald found himself quailing, and stuttered and stumbled over his description of his embarrassingly vague and elusive symptoms. When he had finished the doctor gave him a protracted neurological examination of clinical savagery, after which a dead silence prevailed as he scribbled away for several minutes. Finally he leaned back in his chair and began tapping the desk with his expensive ballpoint, staring at Donald disconcertingly.

'Partly, I think,' said Dr Conradi at last, spreading his hands on his desk in an expansive gesture, 'what you are experiencing has to do with the kind of person you are. You are an advocate, Mr Humbie: you are used to dissecting situations and analysing them minutely. You are sensitive to peculiarities of all sorts. If you weren't, you wouldn't be able to do your job properly. You are, perhaps, keenly aware of certain sensations which others might scarcely notice, possibly not be aware of at all.' He raised his hands with the palms facing each other, his elbows resting on the arms of his chair, and went on:

'If we were to imagine a scale of awareness of our bodily sensations, with everyone, you see, at a different point of the scale . . . ' and here he even drew a little sketch with his ballpoint pen upon his blotting-pad . . . 'you might perhaps be found towards the upper end of that scale.' Dr Conradi had, he clearly felt, spoken with great finesse, and was modestly pleased with the tactful urbanity with which he had found a way to be almost complimentary about what he no doubt considered Donald's morbid hypochondria.

'You mean I'm imagining it all?' Donald blurted out.

The doctor gave a start: he looked hurt, even slightly shocked. But he quickly pulled himself together and looked his patient straight in the eye:

'That would be to put it more crudely than I would wish.'

'Either I am imagining my symptoms or I am not,' Donald replied patiently. 'If they have any objective basis whatsoever, however slight, then I am not imagining them. If they have not, then I am, and to say so would not be crude but merely factual.'

'Would it were that simple . . . ' the doctor murmured as if to himself, and almost pityingly; then as it were brushed this weakness aside and abruptly altered his tactics.

'I can find nothing wrong with you,' he stated bluntly. 'What you have described is subjective experiences.'

'All experiences are of their nature subjective,' Donald countered with dogged adroitness. 'That which, *qua* experience, is subjective, may, however, have an objective causation.'

'In this case I can detect none.'

'One may, nonetheless, exist – one which is not presently detectable.'

The doctor stared at Donald impassively.

'One thing I can tell you with 100% certainty,' he said. 'Not with 80% or 90% certainty, but with 100% certainty.'

Donald forebore to observe that certainty was of its nature 100%, and could not be less.

'With 100% certainty,' the doctor reiterated needlessly. 'You do not have Friedrich's Ataxia.'

Donald's heart lunged down somewhere towards his boots before steadying itself. Since he had never for a moment entertained or suggested the possibility that he had Friedrich's Ataxia, why should Dr Conradi have felt it necessary to refute the possibility of such a diagnosis, unless it were precisely Friedrich's Ataxia that his description of his symptoms had suggested to him?

But he could scarcely say that.

'You think I'm neurotic?' he asked instead.

'If you're suggesting that, I won't contradict you,' the doctor replied; and with that the consultation came to an end.

'Do you think I'm neurotic?' Donald asked Peter when he got back to the cottage.

The detective laughed in his friendly but rather non-committal way. 'We're all neurotic, right enough. That's got nothing to do with it, really. The question is more whether you're delusional.'

Donald was somewhat taken aback by his directness:

'Well? Do *you* think I'm delusional?'

'No,' said MacNucator slowly. 'I don't think that. Not delusional. I don't think so.'

9

Alexandria

'You're going to have to be patient,' said the detective
with great firmness. 'I believe I can help you, but it's
going to take time. These people have inveigled you into
their web, and we can extract you only by applying our
wits to the business.'

Donald gazed at MacNucator in dismay. They were
sitting opposite one another in the cosy little sitting-room,
the advocate reclining on an ancient sofa, the detective
sunk deep in his armchair by the peat fire, the tips of
his thin, strong fingers resting lightly on their opposite
numbers, his grey eyes fixed steadily on Donald yet at
the same time inwardly directed. Donald had formed, as
yet, little idea of what kind of a man he was. A bachelor,
it seemed, or at least currently wifeless, with tidy habits;
about sixty years old; native to the area; frugal in disposi-
tion and even more frugal in the information he imparted
about himself.

In the little bookshelf beside his chair to the right of the fireplace were books about fishing and the hills, folk-lore, a few nineteenth-century novels, and an abundance of maps. Ordnance Survey maps, sea charts, and, inter-estingly enough, maps of foreign places. There were no detective stories. A little notebook always to hand, in which he wrote from time to time, as they talked, with an old stub of a pencil. Between them on the table a pot of coffee. So they were to sit for an hour or two every day for quite a few days to come. Sometimes they would go walking together, sometimes each wanted to be on his own. But Peter's time, as he had made clear, was at his client's disposal for as long as should prove necessary.

'But . . . Madeleine!' Donald cried in alarm. 'I can be patient for myself, but my wife is in peril! We have to find out what they've done with her! For God's sake, Peter,' he groaned and buried his face in his hands – 'I've got to face the possibility: they may even have killed her!' His face was wild and terror-stricken.

'I don't think so,' said MacNucator with great calm-ness. 'They're concerned with you, not with her. Mad-eleine, to them, is just a means of getting at you. You can be confident of that. You see, if they killed her they would have done their worst – so then they would have no more hold over you.'

'Oh, God! How can I possibly be sure of that? We must try to get in contact with her – find her! Surely we must do that?'

MacNucator shook his head in a way that brooked no disagreement. 'That would be playing into their hands. That was how you got into their clutches in the first place, wasn't it? When you phoned home, and got Motion's message? Yes, indeed. No, no, Donald, that's not the way. You must trust me on that. Madeleine will be all right. Believe me. Besides . . . we're very remote, here, you know. Communications aren't easy.'

'You must surely have phones?'

'Yes, we have phones, right enough. But usually they don't work.'

Donald gaped. What could one possibly reply to that?

'Tell me,' said the detective, laughing and scratching his head and tacitly pushing that line of discussion aside, 'what did you make of that show of theirs? I mean, what was the point of it, would you say? Was it funny? Witty? Clever, profound in any way?'

'Not in the least. It had no real substance at all. It was silly and vulgar in the extreme. I don't mean smutty or dirty, particularly − just vulgar − cheap. Pretentious and irredeemably second-rate.'

'So what would you say was the point of it?'

'To get at me!'

'And did it succeed in that, would you say?'

Donald was momentarily nonplussed. 'Well, it made me angry, naturally. But I gave them a piece of my mind all right, I can tell you! Oh, I didn't miss them, I can tell you that!'

'Which was just what they wanted, of course,' said Peter equably, pouring more coffee. 'So they were taunting you, were they? Enjoying watching you angry and confused, not knowing what it was you were facing? Was that how it was? Was that how you felt?'

'Yes, that was it! That was the way I was feeling.'

'What was the nature of their power over you, would you say?'

'Well, they had my wife, of course! Or they pretended they did. They wanted me to think that she'd joined them. That they'd succeeded in taking her away from me, snatching away the woman I love.'

'And Mrs Macrae too? They'd taken her away also?'

'Yes – yes, that's true.' Donald felt a wave of something like despair pass over him. He didn't quite know why the disappearance of Mrs Macrae made it so much worse; but it was as if *everything* had been snatched from him, not just Madeleine but the whole familiar basis of his life, the whole context in which he could feel loved and secure. The creeping panic of the day he had come to Fliuchary invaded him anew.

MacNucator perceived his disturbance and shifted the line of his enquiry once more. 'How would you characterize these people, Donald?' he asked, his face turned to the steadily smouldering fire. 'What sort of a feel did they have for you?'

'Well, they were malicious,' said Donald, conceptualizing his impressions with difficulty as he went along. 'Yet they were vacuous as well. There was a kind of emptiness at the heart of them, I'd say. Almost like psychopaths. They were very threatening, but it was hard to take them altogether seriously, all the same. They meant what they were doing seriously, don't mistake me, and it was working, yet . . . '

MacNucator turned and looked at him, nodding repeatedly, pleased and, Donald thought, impressed by this reply.

'Yes, my friend, you've put your finger on it. These people, you see – what are they? Actors, impersonators, impostors: usurpers, as you've said. Yes, perhaps that too. They have no fixity, they are always changing shape, their characters are only half-formed. They are less real than we are. They have only a limited kind of reality. We humans, of course, we *all* have a limited degree of reality – in that we are less real than God, I mean. Our reality is of a dependent kind. But these people, this Sinister Cabaret, their calling has robbed them of some of the reality they should possess. And it's that which gives us our opportunity. Because they only have as much power as we allow them.'

'Well, that's a comforting thought,' said Donald, not quite sure whether or not he meant it ironically.

'But don't mistake me,' the detective at once came back. 'That doesn't mean that they are not dangerous. They can do you a great deal of damage, even to the point of fatality. Because even though, as I say, they have only as much power as we allow them, it's no easy matter to break the hold that they have already established. In fact, it's very hard indeed. You have a struggle on your hands, Donald: I don't want to conceal it. I make no claim that this is going to be easy.'

'Well, what are we going to do? You haven't said anything about that yet. We'll have to take some positive measures. If we're not going to call in the police – and I confess I'm not keen on that idea myself, that's why I came to you, after all – we must at least gather some evidence against them.'

'Oh, we will do that, right enough, but not quite in the usual way. We can only reach them through you. I can't quite explain that right at this moment, because I think we're both tired. But tomorrow I want to tell you something about Alexandria. Yes, I think we'll start our journey in Alexandria.'

'Alexandria? The city in Egypt?'

'The same.'

'What on earth do you mean?'

'You'll see soon enough.'

It was one of MacNucator's little foibles to take pleasure in being provocatively enigmatic, and Donald saw that he must possess his soul in patience.

That evening, after dark had fallen, the detective and his client took a walk along the northern shore of the long sea loch at the head of which Cul an Duirn was situated, where there was no paved road but only a rough track. The night was dry, bright and frosty but there was no moon. They walked almost in silence, each wrapped in his own thoughts, yet with an unspoken mutual sympathy informing their lack of words, born less of natural affinity than of the exacting frankness of the exchanges which had taken place between them in the past days, which had issued in a certain reciprocal trust and respect.

Donald was gazing out to where the mouth of the loch merged with the sea when he became aware of a strange, shifting effulgence on the undisturbed face of the water. Looking up he saw, with less astonishment than awe and wonder, a huge object in the sky like the outline of a horse, drawn with stars but shining with a more than starlike light. It had tiny sickle moons for ears and planets for eyes, and luminous threads of milky vapour seemed to trail between the stars that composed the outline, like the pencil lines which join up the dots on a children's picture puzzle. It reminded Donald irresistibly of a cave painting. The horse was moving in a great arc across the sky, a thing from beyond this world, numinous and awe-inspiring. Donald touched Peter's sleeve and pointed, and together they gazed at it in silence.

'What is it?' Donald whispered at last.

'I don't exactly know. But it's something to do with the journey you have to make. Something to keep in mind while you're travelling. Perhaps even the object of your search.'

As they watched, the starry horse, gradually growing fainter as its course descended towards the south, dropped below the horizon and disappeared.

It was after they had been having a drink or two in the Mountain Dew that MacNucator told Donald what he had been meaning about Alexandria. The detective and his client went now and again to this eccentric but altogether likeable howff for a couple of whiskies after their discussions, but were always careful not to overdo it. There were quite enough people overdoing it in the Mountain Dew as it was. The pub life there was comfortingly regular and predictable. Every evening Arkady Vasilyevich Pachydermatov bewailed his fate, cadged drinks and wept floods of tears over Mother Russia, Anastasia Ignatyevna and his little Sofia Arkadyevna, but flirted incorrigibly all the same with Ingibjorg Sigurdsdottir, who invariably repulsed his advances. Big Hieronymus wandered blearily around the bar swearing incomprehensibly in Dutch and annoying customers by thrusting his face into theirs and attempting to speak to them. People fell down, smashed glasses, broke chairs over each other's heads and urinated in their trousers; and Kenny Squeezebox, always wearily philosophical, knocked their skulls together or picked them up like sacks of oats and threw them bodily out on to the pavement.

But for all the little dissensions there was an unmistakable if tacit freemasonry among the denizens of the Mountain Dew. They would stand up for each other against any outsider; anyone could readily see that. And Donald had early come to realize that they treated Peter MacNucator with a respect that bounded on awe, though it was not altogether clear why. The detective stood far above all the feuds, quarrels and vendettas which routinely breached the hostelry's peace and was regarded as a figure of learning, experience and authority.

Any friend of Peter's was considered to be all right, so it was not too long before Donald began to feel that he too had been accepted, if not without proper caution. In spite of all the ructions and commotion he felt remarkably at ease in the Mountain Dew; the only thing which caused him a painful and recurring disturbance was, of course, the poster announcing the coming appearance of the Sinister Cabaret, at this moment barely a week away.

Now the pair were adding a malt in front of the fire to the two or three they had put away in the Mountain Dew. Peter was in a comfortable, armchair mood; in no hurry, it seemed, to get to the point Donald was so curious about.

'So,' the latter prompted him impatiently, 'what's this you were going to tell me about Alexandria?'

'Ah, Alexandria! Well, it's just a little analogy, you see, almost just a wee joke in its way. Yes. The fact is, so I believe, that the present city may one day simply collapse, disappear altogether into its past without leaving a trace.'

'Disappear into its past? You're being mysterious again. Make it plain to me.'

'Well, I meant it pretty literally, as it happens. You see, the present city of Alexandria is built directly on top of the ancient one. Nothing so unusual about that, I suppose, except that a great part of the original is actually still there. Not just the foundations and a few bits of broken rubble, but substantially intact – streets and houses and shops and temples and palaces. Crypts and catacombs too. And what's more, the layer of earth that separates one from the other is rather thin. So it not infrequently happens that holes suddenly open up in streets or the floors of houses, and whoever is unlucky enough to be right above them at the time is simply swallowed up – consumed by the city of the past – and is never seen again.'

'Hmm – very piquant. But you said it was an analogy. What to?'

'Well, Donald, I don't need to tell you that the present lives of all of us are underlaid by our pasts. The past is divided from us by only a thin layer and forms the foundation of our present existence. What's more, it's always trying to suck us in, recover us, gain possession of us once more. We can be sucked in there just like those unfortunate citizens of Alexandria, be overwhelmed and never again emerge. But if we can *find* a way in, search for it and find it, then we can go down there consciously and with a purpose. And then we can do whatever needs to be done down there, and shore up our crumbling foundations. Finally, if we're lucky, we can fight our way back up and into the open air.'

'I see. And that's what you want me to do?'

'Yes. And I want to help you to do it.'

'Okay. So what's the role of the Sinister Cabaret in all this?'

MacNucator leaned back in his chair, took a sip of Lagavoulin and let his eyes wander fitfully about the room while he smiled in his inward manner.

He's up to his little tricks again, Donald thought. He wants me to think that he knows absolutely clearly what the Sinister Cabaret have got to do with it all, but it's going to be so hard to get over to someone of my limited spiritual understanding that he's going to have to ruminate for a bit about how best to present the matter. An analogy, perhaps? A little joke?

The detective, seeming to read his thoughts, sat up straight and stared at him rather sternly.

'I hope you're taking this seriously, boy,' he said like a schoolmaster. 'You know perfectly well what their role is. They're bogeymen – sorry, sorry, bogeypersons I should probably say, these days – personae, masks, shifting projections of your inmost fears. Creatures of limited substance. Which is not to say that they're not real. If they weren't real you wouldn't be in deep trouble, which you undoubtedly are. After all, they're appearing at the village hall in – what? – less than a week, I think. That's not long.'

'So – what do you propose? I'm listening.'

'I propose what I've already suggested. You have to find your way down in there, voluntarily, with purpose. And later you have to get out again. While you're down there, you have to discover what these people represent. It's what they represent, of course, which gives them their power over you. Only when you understand that can you know how to deal with them. And it's very important that you don't try to deal with them on their own terms. If you do that, you may *think* that you've defeated them, but one fine day they'll come bouncing back. No, no – they have to be *disarmed*.'

'But how can I find my way down there? Into this underground past you're talking about? Just by remembering?' Donald was troubled.

'Not just by remembering. It's the use you make of your memories that counts. And first *you* have to be disarmed too. Don't worry, I'll deal with that.'

'I don't think I understand what you're saying.'

'Never mind about that. Look, here's a trick that you can try. Think of some places that have been important in your life. Think how they are now. Have they changed since they first became important to you? Almost certainly. Maybe only a little, maybe a lot. But certainly they've changed in some essential way, inwardly if not on the surface. All right, think about them as they are now. Then imagine that, just as in Alexandria, their old self is lying somewhere beneath the surface. Not that far down either. Right – you've got to go down in there. But don't let yourself fall. You have to dive. Don't worry, you won't crack your skull. The past is a fluid substance.'

Donald was invaded by a deep terror, almost to the point of panic. It was as if a perilous journey for which he had hoped to make a long preparation had been brought forward quite without warning and he had to set off, totally unprepared, straight away.

'But . . . where on earth do I know where to start?' he faltered. 'Please don't say at the beginning.'

The detective laughed. 'Oh no, I won't say that. But

what would you say the Cabaret's immediate hold over you is? What is it that you have to fear from them?'

'Well, obviously . . . They claim to have taken my wife away. I don't know what they have done with Madeleine. I'm even afraid they may have killed her.'

'Right, then. Begin with Madeleine.'

10

Cities of the Past

'Don't worry,' said Malcolm Griffin. 'She'll come round in due course.'

Donald had followed MacNucator's instructions and now he was sitting, one evening about thirty years back, in the Café Royal in Edinburgh with this older advocate who had rather taken him under his wing. Malcolm Griffin was a thin, wiry man with a little wizened face and a fund of worldly wisdom which he liked to impart to the younger generation in a tone of detached but friendly cynicism, though he probably thought of it rather as realism. He was a man always on the peripheries, not altogether accepted by the legal establishment, partly because of some hazy rumours about his past, and more so because of his Nationalist commitment. Donald thought him capable of violence and felt an obscure excitement in his company.

The day before, Madeleine had rejected Donald's proposal of marriage and he was now in the depths of despair. Everything seemed different, the familiar scenes and kent faces around him somehow robbed of their reality, just as he felt himself robbed of his own central reality, not so much by that symbolic other person whose existence was dividing him from Madeleine – someone who seemed to come and go in her life without rhyme or reason; not so much by him as by life itself. He was surprised, in a way, how he was at all able to carry on with life in the normal fashion, how he came to be sitting here on his accustomed bar stool at the usual hour, chatting to Malcolm Griffin. Though certainly it hadn't been quite their usual kind of chat. He didn't quite know why he had confided in Griffin, who wasn't the sort of person to whom he would normally have opened his heart, but he was ready to grab at straws, and the older man's prediction that she would 'come round in due course' gave his heart a tiny lift in spite of his resolve not to allow himself false consolation.

'You really think so?' he asked, trying not to sound too eager.

'Oh yes. She just needs time to see it from a different angle, you see. Then she'll realize that she's always loved you, but that she was fighting it. That's what she'll say.'

'You take a very cynical attitude,' said Donald. 'I can't take that kind of a view.'

'You're young yet,' replied Griffin with an odd little laugh. 'You will.'

'Madeleine's nothing if not honest with herself, I'm afraid. Almost unpleasantly high-minded at times, in fact.'

'Oh,' said Griffin, 'I'm not being cynical about Madeleine personally, you know. No more than about any woman – any human being come to that, though I must say . . . no, I won't say.' He changed his tactics and adopted a gentler tone – that of a kindly and experienced uncle:

'You can be honest with yourself without actually knowing yourself, you see. You've probably given her a shock. Give her a chance, allow her time to see things in a different light, that's the thing to do. You can even suggest to her in what light she might see them – not too directly, mind you, just plant the seed. "Except a seed fall into the ground and die . . . " Then all you have to do is stick around. Just stick around. Not all the time, of course. You should disappear sometimes too. Then she'll learn how to miss you. She'll come round, don't worry. Maybe in a couple of months, maybe in ten years, but she'll come round.'

Donald laughed out loud and bitterly.

'Oh, don't laugh,' said Malcolm very seriously. 'You have to be constant. Most people take a short-term view of these things. They play a short game. Anyone can do that. Sometimes they lose and sometimes they win, but then either way they lose interest and it all falls to pieces. The long game requires more intelligence, and also more character. But the loser now will be later to win, as our friend says.' He paused and his tone became bleaker again. 'What, on the other hand, is winning? "Ireland will have her freedom and you still break stones." '

'Yeats?'

'Yes.' He stared off across the bar. 'Still, at least one has won.' He started to giggle in an odd way he had that sometimes threatened to become hysterical. But then he recovered himself and continued:

'It's a long game, Donald. Just stick around. It's the

same with Scotland, with independence. People in the SNP see us winning all these seats and they imagine it'll all be over in a couple of years. It won't. Others again are convinced that it will never happen. They're both wrong. It's a long game. It takes people a long time to see things in a different light. But things change and it comes to be to their advantage to see things differently. It'll be a long time yet before they all discover that they were really nationalists all along. But it'll happen, mark my words!'

'So you're of the considered opinion that I shouldn't give up hope?' asked Donald, pointedly ignoring a know-all legal apprentice who had sauntered up while they were talking and was shamelessly listening in to their conversation, puffing away affectedly at a cigarette, with a sceptical look on his face. This Hugh Anderson was always trying to impress Griffin with his supposedly searching intelligence and superior worldly wisdom, when in fact he had a remarkably commonplace mind. Griffin gave him one of his measured and ambiguous looks through narrowed, hooded eyelids. He didn't like this interruption and perhaps feared that his judgment was about to be questioned.

'Uhm . . . Oh, no, never give up hope,' he replied to Donald rather weakly, and drained his pint glass.

'Excuse my nasty habit of eavesdropping,' put in Hugh Anderson, 'but am I right in understanding, from what I've just heard, that Madeleine's given you the bum's rush, Donald? – if you don't mind my way of putting it.'

'It's a bit late for you to try and find out if I mind it or not. But, however that may be, the answer to your question is yes.'

'Well, don't hang around, that's my advice, even if it's

the opposite to Malcolm's. Romantic ideals won't do you any good. Constancy, faithfulness, undying love – none of that's going to do you any good. Forget all that. Move on, Donald. Move on.' Anderson had the irritating habit of holding his glass and his cigarette in the same hand, in a manner he thought extremely urbane, while the other held his folded newspaper; he would pretend to be studying the crossword puzzle while he eavesdropped.

Donald didn't bother to reply but stared at Hugh as if he would have liked to squash him underfoot, which indeed he would.

But Hugh didn't like to be ignored. 'Are you an idealist or a realist?' he almost shouted in his annoyance. 'That's the question. Do you want to be an idealist or a realist?'

'I can see no reason why I shouldn't be both,' replied Donald coolly.

'Because they're opposites, that's why! You can't be both at once.'

'Oh yes, I can. As a matter of fact I do it every day. – I'll probably see you tomorrow, Malcolm.' Donald finished his drink and left the bar.

Something had just struck him: what he had said in response to Hugh Anderson's mediocre cynicism and meretricious worldly wisdom, which had come straight off his tongue without thought and was entirely motivated by animus, was in fact nothing but the truth. The real and the ideal were not opposites, and only an irredeemably mediocre and commonplace mind could think of them as such. What such minds called 'real' was not real at all: it was a passing charade lacking value or substance or permanence, and at the end of the day a delusion. True reality was to be sought elsewhere; true reality was to be created. It was a catalyst to transform life. He knew that he couldn't express this idea in a way that would have convinced Hugh Anderson or perhaps anyone else; but he knew too that he had been granted, and possessed by, an insight which would sustain him through many difficulties. It was to be longer than Griffin's ten years that he was to wait for Madeleine, and it sustained him all that time.

The present Donald left the pub along with the younger one and wandered through the city of the past, wholly in the possession of a sense of overwhelming grief and loss. As in all the years gone by, a wind was blowing through the city; but this time it was the redolent wind of memory, wistful and enchanting. All around him were the sights and sounds and smells of thirty years ago. The old pubs and the old streets and the old faces, many of those last now gone for ever. Many of the pubs and the streets too, come to that. The pubs now all gutted and refitted, become glitzy and thematic and vulgar; utterly alien. The streets, some of them, unrecognizable; or else altogether dissolved as if they had never been, not a rack left behind. The familiar faces, loved, liked, disliked or none of these: unique, irreplaceable faces, forgotten but now remembered, faces claimed and dissolved by death, by thirty years of death and devolution.

The city of the past haunting the city of the present; the past Donald haunting his present self. The area around the university, once dismantled bit by bit, now reconfiguring itself as he strode up the Mound and down deeper into the past. Bristo; Parker's Stores, where his mother bought elastic for his stocking garters when he was a schoolboy. George Square, with its old, elusive, unreachable sense

of depth and history, unappreciated back in the dim old
fifties; Charles Street and the Paperback bookshop, with
its stuffed rhinoceros head on the pavement – where, as
a law student grieving for his lost vocation as a writer,
he would lose himself in Beckett and the French *nouvelle
vague* and fall briefly in love with Eastern mysticism.

Marshall Street and Lothian Street, rearing once more
their dark tenement heads; through a door and into the
Crown, and there he was in the midst of his first passion
for Madeleine. Her hand grasping his for the first time
under a table there; his lips reaching for hers in the car
outside. Walking home up to Comiston in the dawn after
being with her; washing their faces on Arthur's Seat in
the May Day dew. His present grief for that past mingling
with the past grief of her loss. The poem that had for long
years been his motto:

> *Unhappie is the man for evirmair*
> *That teils the sand and sawis in the aire;*
> *Bot twyse unhappier is he, I lairn,*
> *That feidis in his hairt a mad desyre,*
> *And follows on a woman throw the fyre,*
> *Led be a blind and teichit be a bairn.*

So long ago.

But all of this was only the top layer. The city of his past
went much deeper than that. And down below, Donald
knew all too well, there were further losses to be sustained.
Deeper, and much longer ago. As deep and as long ago as
the dawn of life. Here indeed was no continuing city.

He had an overwhelming sense now, suddenly, of life
not as a linear journey from birth to death, but as an

elliptical journey out and back: out from and back in the direction of its source. What Griffin had said to him that day had helped him to keep going forward, to the point where he got, at last, the woman he loved. Yes, that must have been the high point of his life, the furthest station on the outward journey. At the time, certainly, he had been very far from understanding that. It was only in retrospect that one could say: Yes, that was the high point, that was the centre. But he saw now that he had already been travelling back towards the source for a long time.

And now he found himself telling all this to Mac-Nucator.

'Oh yes,' said the detective, 'there's a time when you have to start going back. You see, when you reach the high point you pause for a little, you think you've got plenty of time, you're at your leisure, you can look around at the view. Then when you've looked around enough and you decide to set out again, you don't realize at first in what direction you're going. Because at first the reverse movement is all but imperceptible: it still feels like going forward. There are still goals ahead, after all! You, for instance, might still be raised to the Bench, eh?' he suggested cunningly.

'Stranger things have happened,' Donald conceded with a grimace.

'Quite. But you see, all that is only on the surface. Deep down, you're already on the journey home.'

'Regression,' said Donald bleakly. 'What a depressing outlook!'

But Peter shook his head very decidedly:

'You misunderstand me. It's not at all a question of regression, not a matter of being possessed by the past, swallowed up by it. I don't deny that that is a danger. Oh, no, I don't deny that – because that's where the Sinister Cabaret come in. What I'm talking about, though, is the opposite. I'm talking about reclaiming the past, *re*-possessing it, or rather possessing it truly for the first time. Only when the past has been reclaimed will it deliver up its inner meaning.'

An obscure terror took hold of Donald's soul. 'I'm not sure that I'm ready. I'm not sure that I can face that yet.'

'You must. You have to go back. If you don't accept that, you will be endlessly torn by an unknown, unacknowledged anguish. And remember: the past can be reclaimed only when it is accepted, only when it is loved, whether in itself it was good or bad.'

11

Lord of the Lies

Cant stood astride the drive with his arms folded. Waiting in the late October dusk. Waiting for the ten-year-old Donald to walk back up the drive to the school building. Towards the brooding walls of this school sixty miles from home, walking very slowly up the wooded drive in the chill Fife air that smelt different from the air of home. Walking very slowly because he didn't want to reach Cant and couldn't avoid him, for skulking at intervals in the shadows other figures could be dimly seen, lurking to cut off any escape route: Pugsie and Big Scrote and Peter Jopp and the rest of Cant's gang, some of them with stones tied inside handkerchiefs to form coshes.

Cant stood waiting patiently with his arms folded. Cant could afford to wait. There was no reason why he shouldn't be patient.

The ghostly figures moved among the trees. Donald knew they weren't ghosts, but Fat MacGillveray hadn't known: or not until Donald had told him. That had been his crime – he had betrayed the ghost conspiracy. Every evening at dusk his fat, sensitive, impressionable friend had to walk down that dark, gloomy, and at this time of year really quite sinister drive: to go home. He was a day-boy, but because his mother was a widow, and worked late, he couldn't go home with the other day-boys at four o' clock but had to stay at school with the boarders for another two hours. Hallowe'en was approaching and Cant had concocted this story about the ghost which had been seen hovering in the earth dug-outs among the trees, just in order to strike terror into the heart of Fat MacGillveray.

Tonight a special haunting had been planned, with all kinds of special effects, and it had worked so well that Fat MacGillveray was smitten with utter terror and panic and froze halfway down the drive and could go neither forward nor back. Donald, who had been assigned to accompany him down the drive to stop him turning back before the show reached its climax, watched his friend gibbering with terror, the tears starting to his eyes, stuttering:

'The ghost . . . is it the ghost, Humbie?'

And he had pity on him. 'There isn't any ghost,' he whispered. 'It's all been made up by Cant to scare the shit out of you, so just run down the drive now as fast as you can, as if the shit had really been scared out of you. Go on, run!'

But as soon as he heard that there wasn't a ghost, Fat MacGillveray just sauntered on quite nonchalantly as if he hadn't a care in the world.

There was gratitude for you.

Donald walked on slowly until he stood a few feet in

front of Cant, then he stopped. Cant stared at him with those eyes that had something dead at the back of them. The eyes of a dead pike, perhaps.

'You told him,' he said.

The figures among the trees started to move out from their hiding-places.

'I had to, Cant, he was scared shitless—'

'You little bastard.'

Now that the gang were all around him they were off their guard. Donald saw they were expecting him to plead further and attempt to justify himself, so he turned from Cant and darted to the right past the bicycle shed and took off as fast as his legs could carry him round the back of the building. It was so unexpected that it took the mob a couple of seconds to react and set off in pursuit.

Never in his life had Donald run faster and he never would again. He didn't know where he could hide, but if he just could get into the building perhaps someone in authority – a master or maybe the matron – would happen to be around. Or he could lock himself in a lavatory, which would at least defer the execution of justice. There was no time to think, but somehow fate might help him. He shot round the corner to the back door and there stood Big Scrote, who had simply taken the short way through the house. A second later he felt a dull thud of pain on his shoulder as the first cosh hit him.

'Throw him in the brambles!' cried Pugsie.

He was frogmarched across the lawn to the steep slope where the brambles grew. Scrote yanked his blazer off his shoulders.

'Give it here!' ordered Cant peremptorily. Quite a small

boy, Cant, but one having authority. He went through Donald's pockets: all that was in them was the envelope containing his mother's birthday card. He had bought it in town only that afternoon after a long and loving search and had been about to pop it in the postbox in the boundary wall, which could just be reached by standing in the fork of a tree and stretching over. Cant ripped the envelope open, sniggered and read the message aloud to the assembled gang.

They laughed and snorted.

'Well,' he remarked, 'Mummy won't be getting this.' He threw it in the mud and ground it under his heel.

Donald wondered what Cant's mother was like.

'Throw him in the brambles!' shouted Scrote, who was getting impatient.

'Not just yet,' said Cant. 'First we're going to rub his cock in the mud.'

At the farm, way over beyond the burn, a dog was barking.

It was a hard place to travel in, this underground city of the past. Donald was spent and weary. The detective poured him a large whisky and he sank back in exhaustion.

'And now that bastard's one of the Sinister Cabaret,' he sighed. 'Yet I could almost feel sorry for him. He was a pathetic individual, really. Probably still is.'

'Beware of pity, where the Cabaret's concerned,' the detective responded firmly. 'You're not to think of them that way. You have to make that journey back with love and joy and acceptance, and the Sinister Cabaret are out to prevent your doing that. Be as sorry for Cant as you like, but remember that he's one of them. It's you or them, Donald – don't ever forget that.'

Donald nodded a bit uncertainly.

'How did you come to be an advocate?' MacNucator asked him after they had enjoyed a long, ruminative silence. 'Was that always your intention?'

Donald laughed to himself, though he didn't quite know why. 'It was always my father's intention. And just for that reason it mostly wasn't mine. But it worked out his way in the end. He was a lawyer himself – a solicitor.'

MacNucator stretched out his legs towards the fire.

'Yes,' he nodded. 'It's true that in everything in life (not just in the matter of a career) there's on the one hand the impulse to behave oppositely to one's parents, and on the other there's the tendency to behave the same. *Mutatis mutandis*, of course. The latter is often the stronger and deeper and is inclined to win out in the end. It has a pull like a fatality, you see. Yes, on the precarious tightrope between those poles many of life's acrobatic feats are performed.' Peter nodded to himself profoundly. He was getting into his philosophical, pipe-tapping vein, in response to which Donald always found himself perversely wanting to bring him up short.

'Mainly I became an advocate because I was good with words,' he remarked.

'There are lots of other things you can do with words,' said MacNucator. 'Did you never consider any of the others?'

The little devil! He always managed to hit upon one's weak spots. Donald realized he would have to confess:

'Well, I always wanted to be a writer. Right from the age of seven I wanted to be a writer.'

'So why didn't you become one?'

That was a good question and one which Donald would be hard put to answer. He could scarcely go on blaming Swinger Swann. When he was already quite an established young advocate, Donald had written half a novel. One evening in a pub he had got into conversation with Dr 'Swinger' Swann, of the School of Literary Fashion at the Pictish University of Lesmahagow, and had told him all about his novel. In the atmosphere of warm bonhomie which prevailed that night the old Swinger had enthusiastically offered to read the work in progress and even, if it should seem appropriate, to write about it to a certain publisher of his acquaintance. He had most likely never expected to have to make good his promise and had no doubt already forgotten it when, only a couple of days later, the script had thudded uncompromisingly through his letterbox. In his student days Swinger Swann had been a passionate and eloquent advocate of literary risk-taking and had actually written his doctoral thesis on this subject, becoming such an authority that he could now see a risk of any kind approaching at twenty leagues' distance, and had so far proved successful in avoiding taking even one, all the days of his life.

When the Swinger had run his eye over the half-written novel, Donald smelled to him very suspiciously like a risk. He could sense on his antennae that this author was most unlikely ever to become famous; and even if, through the unpredictable perversity of fate, he ever did, it would almost certainly not be in either of their lifetimes. Should he praise this novel prematurely, Dr Swann's career would lie in ruins!

Yet a promise was a promise, and he was a man of

integrity. Swinger Swann spent a sleepless night tossing and turning and tearing out his eyebrows hair by hair; but in the morning he rose bravely, though clearly exhausted by his inner struggle, and with his eyebrows torn and lacerated, kissed his wife goodbye and drove steadfastly to his office at the Pictish University, where almost without hesitation, almost impetuously, he typed out (even Swinger Swann didn't have a computer in those days) such a masterpiece of evasion, caution and faint praise that it remains a joy to read even unto this very day, or at least would do if it still existed. When Donald pursued the publisher the latter spilled the beans and told him that Dr Swann didn't feel able to recommend the novel 'at this stage' and 'in its present state', which considering that it was only half written was not a revolutionary stance to take. And only-half-written was what it remained.

But Donald had to admit that it probably would have done anyway.

'I had difficulty in finishing things,' he tried to explain, in fact thinking about this consciously for the first time. 'I always started with a rush of enthusiasm, I remember. But after I'd written a few chapters I'd think, "Well, I've said more or less what I had to say, I don't think I can be bothered doing any more of this, really." That's what it mainly was, I think. And I felt that endings were artificial, anyway. That there weren't any real endings in life.'

'It wasn't that you were scared of being rejected?'

Donald dropped his eyes for a moment then looked up at the detective without raising his head.

'There might be something in that too.'

'Maybe you should try to find out.'

Donald felt again that obscure dread and terror. 'I don't like it, this burying myself in the past. I'm not senile yet.'

'It's true that old people do something similar at the very end of their days, but they do it passively and without purpose. I'm asking you to re-possess your past consciously and purposively. And now you need to think about that writing of yours. Because that's another of your losses, isn't it? That vocation?' MacNucator pursued relentlessly. 'Another of the things that you feel were taken away from you?'

'Oh, yes. It's one of those all right.'

12

Juvenilia

Donald was seated just behind the right shoulder of his former self, making himself very quiet and unobtrusive so as not to impede the concentration of the thirteen-year-old author who was labouring away, with many groans and curses, at a huge antiquated typewriter with blotchy, clogged keys, set on a card table with a green baize cover. The typewriter made a tremendous noise and so did the boy's cursings as he repeatedly botched the clear beauty of the paper, even though it was only the reverse side of the letterhead of his father's legal firm. But he was labouring away to good effect.

He was working at a Billy Bunter story. Young Donald knew that Frank Richards, Billy Bunter's creator, was now a very old man, and he had a fantasy. The fantasy was that he would write such a good Billy Bunter story, imitate the master's style to such effect, that he would be appointed his official successor and become the wealthy and distinguished author of a whole string of new adventures of that immortal character, 'the Fat Owl of the Remove'. Donald experienced again, as if the years had never been, the radiance of that promise, his utter immersion in the hope-inspired project. The unseen onlooker had to remind himself continually not to comment, suggest or interfere as, utterly locked away in his private world, the boy laboured on.

Donald went on watching the youthful author (though it must be admitted that he snoozed at times) as he typed out no less than seven chapters of this story. This was one that he had actually finished. And he could see why he should have had ambitions for it, too, because the pastiche of the writer's admittedly highly imitable style was near-perfect. It really was quite difficult to detect that this was not vintage Frank Richards. Donald looked on with something very like pride as his younger self sealed the story up and posted it to the famous author.

Waiting for a response to a manuscript sent out into the great unknown world must be not unlike awaiting the arrival of a longed-for baby. Often, too, the waiting lasts for just about as long. At first one is happy enough to know that the process is under way: there is nothing to be done, after all, and a pleasant enough feeling that the matter is out of one's hands and there is no use worrying too much about the outcome. Life carries on much as before, days and weeks come and go, there are all kinds of everyday matters to attend to, and, besides, a kind of superstitious feeling that it's best not to dwell on a future which is still so uncertain.

You know, all the same, that a process is going on, that something is developing – a 'result' – which will one day emerge into palpable, living form, into tangible reality. So in spite of yourself you find that the imagination is painting happy pictures, drawing glad scenes, elaborating all kinds of splendid fantasies, endowing with all the specificity of detailed, imagined life what is in reality still barely more than potential and absolutely unknown. But the thing that is taking shape is all the while losing its airiness and insubstantiality, the being within is becoming inescapably heavier, as its time draws nearer it begins to assert its reality, and so to cast a shadow of apprehension over the brightly lit hopefulness of the day-dreaming, expectant mind. This thing is real: what will it be? Hero or monster? The fulfilment of one's dearest hopes, or the rude dashing to the ground of the fragile sandcastles of desire?

The boy awaited with growing trepidation the parturition of his imaginative offspring.

Donald was there, observing discreetly, when the packet came back three or four months later, and the boy took it up to his room to open it in private. But he didn't really like to look too closely as his former self read the fateful letter.

The creator of Billy Bunter explained to the 'dear boy' that he was unable to read manuscripts, much as he should like to do so. He was, he confessed, a very old man, and his eyesight so poor that he found it far from easy to read even his own typescripts, which he had to do for purposes of revision: and any addition just couldn't be managed. But it had been very kind of Donald to send the story along, and he wished him every success in writing. There followed, after further kind wishes, the blotted but rather fine signature, which became a treasured keepsake.

A keepsake of the hope that he came to believe had been snatched from him by the arbitrary accident of an old man's blindness.

One of life's earliest defeats.

'The hopes of youth dashed, eh?' said the detective with a hint of amusement, but not unkindly.

Donald sighed. 'Oh, yes! But I think that I must have been losing my freshness of imagination by then anyway. That was pure pastiche, after all. The clouds of glory were gone. My earlier stuff was the real me.'

'No doubt! And that's the quickest way back to your deepest self – the way of the imagination. You're very lucky to have that writing of yours to go back by. Think of it as a tightrope to cross the abyss of time.'

'Ha! Suppose I fall off?'

'If you do, you'll only fall into your self. You have to go there anyway. The tightrope will just save you some arduous journeying in those depths, if you can stay on it. It'll help you to get quicker where you want to go.'

'I suppose I'll have to, then . . . but I'm not enjoying this as much as I hoped I might!'

'You're not supposed to be enjoying it! Work's meant to be hard.'

Donald sighed again, resignedly, and went deeper into the past – two or three years further back. No typewriter then, of course: the boy was bent over his desk writing with a fountain-pen, in a still rather unformed hand, in an exercise-book. Concentrating hard and writing quite fast. Writing pastiche already; pastiche, it appeared, of Sir Walter Scott. The Wizard of the North. This is how it went:

Cavalier Downie: A Story of 1649

In the year 1649 England was in a turmoil. King Charles I, having completely ruined his cause, was dead, but still many of his side clung to the hope that the young Prince Charles, only nineteen, would one day succeed to his father's throne. The country was still in a terrible state following six years' war, and the battles of Marston Moor, Naseby, and others, had left it with a smaller population, no well-settled form of government, and internal strife still raging despite the firm hand with which Cromwell ruled the land. Prince Charles had made numerous attempts to avenge his father's death and place himself on the throne. All the Cavaliers supported him, and not a few Roundheads had turned against Cromwell on the King's death, which they considered, perhaps rightly, was going too far. The Ironsides could put down open rebellion against the Commonwealth, but they could not stop leagues being formed to support the youthful Prince. All over the country people of all classes were meeting and forming groups of opposition to the Government, so that Prince Charles, had he wished, could have probably raised quite a considerable army under his standard. All open support, however, was kept well in check.

It is in this year of disorder, then, that our story opens. In northern England, about fifty miles from the town of York, there is a wide expanse of moorland, utterly barren, dreary and uninhabited. It is about ten by eight miles in area, and in all that wild area only about five cottages are found. In 1649 it was crossed by one solitary road, rocky and stony, and only wide enough for one horse to ride along it. It traverses this desert waste from the town of Ardlethwaite in the north to Navedale in the south. It commands a good view: to the north-west and west loom the mountains of the English Lake District; to the north can distantly be seen the hills of the Borders on a fine day; to the east and the south-east lies the Pennine Chain. To the south the more fertile and habitable tracts of Southern Yorkshire.

One day in the early spring of 1649, a solitary traveller rode on horseback across this wild country along the narrow path. He was probably about thirty-five or forty years of age, and bore himself well on his beautiful horse. He wore a large, flowing brown wig, and had sharp and handsome, almost cruel features, and brown eyes which looked as if they could see through anyone's thoughts. He was dressed in a leathern doublet, which showed beneath a navy blue velvet jacket with gold buttons. He wore a piece of lace at his neck, and at his side hung a sword. Riding breeches and boots, together with hawking gloves, completed his attire. His face was stained with blood, and he appeared to have been in a skirmish, probably fighting for the Cavaliers, for his noble dress and looks told as much. He appeared to be wandering aimlessly on, and was obviously a stranger to the district.

'Curse this infernal country!' he said to himself. 'Is there no cottage on the whole of this damnèd moor? Methinks I will have to spend another night out of doors if one comes not in sight soon. It must still be at least thirty miles to the manor.'

Thus gloomily he rode along for another ten minutes or so, until he suddenly stopped, and peering into

the gathering gloom (for it was late at night), he said,
'Beshrew me if that be not a small holding. Perhaps I
will receive hospitality there, but it is yet a long way
off.'

With these words he spurred his horse so that it ran
at the nearest approach to a gallop which the stony road
permitted. But after some minutes the beast whinnied
and fell lame, for it had dashed its hoof against a rock.
Cursing, the rider dismounted and bent to examine the
injury. But even as he did so he heard muffled footsteps.
He whirled round, and saw a frightful-looking creature
leap from behind a bush. It was dressed from head
to heel in red, and wore a leathern jacket and cloth
breeches. Its face was brown and pock-marked, with
a broken nose and dark blue eyes, the forehead was
battered, and the chin – well there wasn't any chin to
speak of. It was no more than four feet six inches in
height, and the left arm was twisted. Indeed he was one
of the most fearsome-looking footpads the first half of the
seventeenth century had seen. Before the Cavalier could
collect himself, the creature stepped forward and dealt
him such a blow with a branch of a tree that he fell on
the ground for dead . . .

Hmm – not bad, thought Donald with some sense of
complacency. If I could write like that when I was eleven,
why the devil am I an advocate now, instead of, let's
say, some obscure novelist? He put this thought to Mac-
Nucator, but the detective seemed less interested in the
precocity of his syntax than in the sudden materialization
of the less-than-comely footpad.

'An early appearance of the Sinister Cabaret, I'd say.

Wouldn't you? Who is this dreadful creature, would you say, who leaps out all of a sudden from behind a bush? Here's a fine, handsome Cavalier riding along, quite the thing – a bit bloodstained, a wee bit battle-weary, I grant you, but quite the thing right enough. A noble-minded, well dressed fellow, though we do notice there's a hint of cruelty in his features . . . What's that doing there, eh? Still, he's riding along quite the thing. Then from behind a bush a hideous apparition rushes out without warning and thumps him on the heid. Sounds as if you had it in for that splendid Cavalier, doesn't it?'

'As the Cabaret have it in for me, are you suggesting?'

'Thou hast said it. So what happens next?'

'Nothing, I'm afraid . . . I didn't finish it.'

'No doubt you'd said what you wanted to. You'd brought the footpad on to centre-stage, hadn't you? And that was a brave thing to do, although you didn't quite know it. Because he's a dangerous fellow, you see, that footpad. Oh, there's no end to the tricks that fellow is up to. He's the one who makes highly moral and respectable, middle-aged family men run away with tarts, for instance. Just as an example. Among many others. I expect we'll see a bit more of that fellow if we go further back. Why don't we do that?'

So back Donald went, not so far this time, perhaps just a few months; and there the boy was again, at his desk once more, scribbling furiously away. In a state, it seemed, of inspiration. Totally immersed in a doleful tale, a tale without a name. Headed only:

Chapter 1

Not very long ago, ten or fifteen years after the First
World War, there were a number of hermit-misers living
in solitary shacks over the British Isles. After a period
of a few years, however, they began, very gradually,
to die out.

One of these lived in a particularly filthy hut in a
clearing of a wood in the lowlands of Scotland, and it
is to him that this story relates. His name was Hezekiah
Lynch, a man who had been left a huge fortune by his
father Gabriel, a thief. Some said that his fortune at one
time amounted to over £850,000. He kept this in a huge
strong-box under the floor of his filthy shack, and his
bed was on the boards which raised to reveal his hoard.
At crack of dawn he used to rise, put on his tattered coat,
and go out to beg.

He had a son, Leonard, who was an invalid, ill with
consumption. He lay bed-ridden, locked in a room adjoin-
ing his father's, getting only a small amount of food to
eat, and that was stolen from shops in the nearby towns.
He was a boy of talent and brain, however, and in his
leisure hours, while he still had the strength, wrote a book
telling of the wretched life of his father, which he hoped
some day to give to some passer-by, accompanied by a
letter to the police advising them to arrest his father as
the foulest thief and vagabond for miles around.

The one other occupant of the house was a wretched
dog, flee-bitten and mangey, who lay all day over its
master's money, and was a superb watch-dog. Ill fared
it with the trousers of him who ventured into that house
while 'Rat-catcher' was about. It was, though, an affec-

tionate brute, with a liking for the young man and children, and a loathing for its master.

Hezekiah Lynch was well-known in the town. He used to go to every door in the town daily, and, whether because they were terrified of him, or, perhaps, to get rid of him and his foul smells of sweat and filth, the housewives always gave him a shilling or two, and often at night he returned to his shack with as much as £8, or even £10. Thus daily his fortune mounted. He had never been known to spend as much as a farthing, and stole, before the very eyes of the terrified assistants, his day's food and a loaf for his son, and ate his portion on the spot. Not one soul knew that he had, in his shack, a son slowly dying of tuberculosis. At night, he used to go to a favourite public house and drink himself into unconsciousness. And if he was given not the spirits free, he always had a stout stick to wield over the back of the unfortunate bar-boy. Very often he lay there all night in a drunken stupor, or reached home at about midnight, there to deposit his day's 'earnings'.

The conditions in the hovel were repulsive. Everything was filth. The old man himself must be described. He was about sixty-five years of age, over six feet in height, and thin as a rake. He had a long, matted grey beard, stuck together with dried egg yolk, soup and other food. His sparse grey hair came over his ears, and his beak nose stuck out like a vulture's. He was covered with lice, as he had never had a bath for twenty-eight years. He wore foul, tattered clothes. His son, a youth of about twenty-five, made some attempt to keep himself clean, and staggered once a week to wash himself in a nearby stream.

Something must be known of this man's family. His father was the youngest of eight children, come from a well-to-do family descended from Norman barons. He was, however, the black sheep of the family, and ran away to sea when he was fifteen. He served in the Navy with little distinction for eleven years, then returned home, and became a thief, the most famous in southern Scotland. He had been left £50,000 by his father, had earned £20,000 in the Navy, and when he became a thief stole another £700,000. He fell in love and married a beggar-woman, who, like her son, saved her beggings, and amassed £50,000. It was such an unhappy marriage, however, that Gabriel Lynch became worn out, and, with the police on his trail and his wife nagging at him, put his head in a gas oven.

Two months after his death his son, the subject of our story, was born, and christened Hezekiah after Lord Lynch, his great-grandfather. His mother died when he was fifteen, and he took the whole of his parents' huge fortune, and built a hovel where he lived for years and years, begging. When he was twenty-nine, he married a rich and clever laird's daughter from nearby. The son, Leonard, was soon after born, and when the child was five Lynch chopped his wife's head off while in a temper and flung her in a pit. Seventeen years later Leonard developed consumption. Hezekiah had been begging for nearly fifty years now, and amassing his fortune. The rest may be left to another chapter.

But, alas! – once again 'the rest' never got written. Thinking about it now, Donald could understand why. Was there any reason for the story to continue? The boy had had his satisfaction from describing the bizarre situation, the odd family history, the filth and nastiness of the wretched old man. Now he found he had to do something with it all. But what? What would have been likely to happen? Wouldn't things just have carried on much as they had been doing for another decade or two, until Leonard had died of consumption or Hezekiah of cirrhosis of the liver?

Or suppose Leonard really had succeeded in passing on that letter to the hoped-for passer-by, the letter to the police advising them to arrest his father as the foulest thief and vagabond for miles around – what then? The police would duly have come to arrest Hezekiah, and Leonard, perhaps, would have been removed to hospital. Not very exciting, really. The boy had wanted something much more dramatic to happen, but he didn't know how to get there. Or rather he did, in a way, or at least could have concocted something, but he couldn't be bothered making the effort that would be involved. The inchoate emotions he had striven to express had found their outlet. So Donald watched as, a month or two later, he went back to his manuscript and contemptuously scrawled out this:

Chapter 2

One day Leonard Lynch found an axe which his father used for chopping wood. When Hezekiah came in, drunk, at night, he waited behind a door, and then cleft his skull with the axe. With the dead brute's fortune he was cured of T.B.

The End

'What do you make of that?' asked Donald a little apprehensively, as the detective was shaking his head slowly from side to side in a provocatively inscrutable style that seemed almost pitying.

'Ends with someone else getting slugged, doesn't it? Just like the last story. But do you notice the difference?'

'Hmm . . . This time the victim's definitely killed?'

'That's true – but who does the killing? That's the point. In the first tale the aggressor is the deformed monster, but here it's the good guy, isn't it? The supposedly virtuous chap, wouldn't you say? The one who's supposed to be the victim – the young man "of talent and brains" . . . wasn't that the phrase? Chops his daddy's head in two with an axe! Not very nice.'

'I suppose not . . . So what do you draw from that, Peter?'

'It's you that has to do the drawing, boy. I'm not going to help you any more from now on. Not for a bit, anyway. You're on your own, Donald. Back you go.'

13

Queenie

As Donald travelled backwards in time on the tightrope of his past imagination, he had a dim apprehension that he was indeed approaching closer, as MacNucator had suggested he would, to where he wanted to be. He needed to be in the world of primordial images, of chaotic emotions, of impulses that were not understood. For that was the world of the Sinister Cabaret: the realm in which its shadowy figures exerted their power over him. If he was to divest them of that power, he knew he had to descend further, deeper into that realm.

He had already moved from a time when the boy stood outside his work, judged its effect, imitated style, exerted a measure of conscious control; from there to a time when he had written from within, gripped by an obscure sense of purpose, a nasty imagination and a love of words, but not quite knowing why he was doing it or where he wanted to go. But it was still a story, and to that degree false.

He must go further back still.

It was becoming easier to do so. That afternoon he and the detective had walked deep into the hills through an evocative dreamlike landscape that strangely reminded him of the way his childhood had been. Not the outward circumstances, but the way it had been within. He was briefly returned to that sweet, dreamlike, elusive world, intolerably sweet, ever hovering on the verge of dissolution. Occasionally throughout his life it had come back to him in swift, unlooked-for flashes, tantalizing glimpses of a lost but perhaps still subsisting world. Now it seemed to be closer, at times to be almost within reach. A time when words themselves had gushed up, not fully understood, from a strange, shadowy, half-formed world full of sad yearning and dim sorrow and wild, undifferentiated feelings . . .

This time the infant prodigy was writing much more slowly, forming the words with difficulty, in big, bold separated letters in dark blue ink. Donald no longer stood apart from him, he could only with difficulty distinguish himself from the boy. As he wrote he shifted from a sitting position and knelt on the chair. On the top right-hand corner of the sheet he wrote the date:

Written: 13th April (Thursday) 1950.

So Donald knew exactly how old he was: eight years and nine months.

After the date he wrote this:

The Damnations of a Man's Life

Part I

We do not often meet, but we
Cannot, do not care.
We cannot say what would be
If we met everywhere.
But find not any fault in that:?
What is there but to do the damnation:
Killed is the man in the sweet nation,
But what is there to do about it?
What is there but to do the damnation's death,
Filled to the heart with deep dissapointment.
A wicked Devil is a king's curse,
Falling on you like a man's devorce,
Striking down the way of force;
But this is not the way of dissapointment,
But the falling of an appointment.
My dying words shall I hope comfort:
Ah! But that I should accomplish!

Part II

The man who is a captain and splutters on your face,
Surely on him a curse will be bestowed:
For he is as a drunkard's fate.
This I know for certain, like the raging wars,
It is nought but the head of a proverb.
But cannot a man's intentions be fulfilled,
Because of a captain who splutters on your face?
That should be too absurd to think,
Oh, May the captain go to Hell!
Like a vile, caressing statue.

Part III

The Emperor is of an evil manner,
For he casteth out his banner,
Crying, 'What can I bestow on the enemie,
But a startled soldier's heart?'
The men who cannot control foul Emperors
Must themselves be considered foul.
Eight times Hell's gates have opened,
Each eight times, eighty people have gone in,
Oh! Eighty and a thousand made of tin.

Meanings of
The Damnations of a Man's Life

While Alexandri Parelli is dying he says in poetry to his servants, this, telling them as it were a parable: It means that when these things happen we have no control over them, and we do not try to stop them, while all the time they are dragging us down further from good to evil. We do not care that we havent put a stop to them. Thus Alexandri Parelli, the dying devil as it were, telling his servants his dying thoughts in poetry.

What, now, was one to make of it all?

A young boy in love with words, in love with rhyme, writing something that he obscurely felt had a meaning but of which he was aware that the meaning was obscure, not least to himself. The meaning lurked somewhere in the rhythms, in the phrases, in the images, in the preoccupations, it skulked in the shadows. And in his curious explication the boy had hit, and certainly not by chance, on the root of what he was writing about: the feeling of helplessness. Of lack of control. We are at the mercy of obscure forces. We know that these things are wrong but we cannot put a stop to them: we are dragged down helplessly from good to evil. The good is lost and evil prevails. That was what this poem was all about. It was also what Donald was feeling about the activities of the Sinister Cabaret.

The Cabaret were set on stealing from him the one he loved most. This awful certainty came on him again with a terrible and inescapable immediacy and almost over-whelmed him, bringing with it an acute sense of panic and helplessness. In a way which he was unable to define (to himself or to the detective), the images of the poem had brought him close to an original feeling of loss, the particularity of which he was almost but not quite able to apprehend.

All at once he teetered on the tightrope and fell through space, plunging into the void of the deep past. When he had recovered his senses he had left the eight-year-old writer far behind and found himself walking once more – shadowing now the steps of a little boy scarcely more than a toddler – through the streets of the under-ground city of the past. Through the gravelled lane which ran between the Episcopal Cathedral and the old music school. Ahead of him across the street lay the oval shape of the wooded gardens behind their iron railings, and he felt his chest constricted by a mingled pressure of terror and love. He knew now what was its source, and as he walked on and gazed over the railings into the garden he was stricken by an upsurging uncontrollable gush of grief and he was racked by bitter sobs.

Queenie! Queenie!

Who was Queenie? Just a wooden horse he had had when he was two years old. A wooden horse on wheels. His constant companion whom he had pushed before him when he walked in the gardens with his mother every morning. Who had been close to him all the time, night and day. The first creature, other than his parents, whom he had invested with love. And whom he had lost.

So what had become of Queenie?

He must have been vaguely aware before of some unfinished business, for he remembered once, years before but when he was already adult, asking his mother that question. Oh, she said, Queenie was never in the new house. At the time they had moved there – when Donald was just three – one of her wheels was broken, his mother thought, and his father had considered her unsafe. Perhaps he had felt that Donald was becoming too attached to her. She didn't remember what had happened to the horse, though; she supposed she had been thrown out, or perhaps given to charity.

Donald had no memory of a moment of parting, no memory of anything about Queenie after the move. Only, now, this aching void of loss and grief, still utterly un-assuaged after half a century and more. He couldn't make sense of it. How could Queenie be unsafe? How could she be thrown out? How could those he loved most and who loved him most have done this to him? And he had had to let it happen – that was the most dreadful thing. That he had had to betray Queenie. That he couldn't save her. Or explain it to her, or tell her he was sorry. That was the most irremediable source of his grief.

All at once there flashed into his mind a picture of the head and neck of a striped wooden horse blackening in the flames of a garden bonfire. But now he was back with her in the crescent gardens, on a spring day sometime in the early 1940s, pushing Queenie before him, in a transport of joy and love, his mother walking by their side. He laughed and ran and Queenie went before him, always responsive, always there just in front of him. As he ran on, everything began to grow dim and fluid and beautiful and shadowy, he seemed to be swimming rather than running, and Queenie had taken the form of a lovely sea-horse. On they went in the watery depths, strange and beautiful fishes and trailing plants and benign sea creatures all about them, amid coloured rocks and sandy grottoes and reefs of glowing coral. For miles they seemed to swim on, unhurried, without purpose or direction, happy just to be together in this luminous dimness, weightless and unharnessed and free, time and space suspended. Donald wanted to go with Queenie further down into the seaweedy depths, to swim there for ever with his hands on her back, in the warm obscurity, in the dim soundless deeps, with the strange shapes and the dim-bright colours all around them. But at last they began to swim up again: he didn't want to go but Queenie was gently pulling him up, up towards the surface and he could only go with her. As they neared the surface Queenie turned her head back towards him with one last look of love, and he knew from that look that she was doing this for him out of love, and out of gratitude because he had truly loved her. As he gazed back at her she surged away, his hands lost their grip, and Queenie plunged, plunged down, down into the depths; and, released, he threw up his arms and hit the surface with a gasp, a great greedy intake of breath, and found himself stretched exhausted on Peter MacNucator's sofa.

So that was what he had been seeking for so long and with so much agony – only a wooden horse!

But no, not just a wooden horse – Queenie.

Queenie whom he had loved.

With, after all, a fragment of the love which pervades all things.

14

Perpetual Motion

'What I don't understand', said Donald to MacNucator as they savoured their now obligatory evening dram a few hours after he had emerged from his salutary ordeal, 'is what Motion has to do with all of this. What am I to him that he pursues me in this way? The others I can understand – at least Cant and Scrote: I have unfinished business with them, you could say, though the business to be done is rather on my side than on theirs, if you want my opinion. But Motion – what is he all about? I don't recall ever meeting him before . . . whenever it was! – my sense of time has gone all haywire recently. Who is he, for God's sake, and what does he want with me?'

The curious little detective scratched his chin reflectively.

Donald couldn't help, in spite of his gratitude, feeling at times that MacNucator was a bit of a poseur.

'These are very difficult questions to answer,' Peter replied, not exactly evasively, but as if loath to say anything which might later prove to be wrong and so reflect poorly upon his professional status. 'It's very hard to say why he pops up just when and where he does. You don't necessarily have to take it personally, any more than when you happen to have caught a rather nasty virus. That's quite a good analogy, in fact, now that I come to think of it: our Mr Motion has a lot in common with a virus.'

'Have you been looking into his background?'

'Oh, I have, I have. But I've seldom had to deal with such an elusive object. Everyone who knows anything about him tells a different story. And hard facts are harder to come by. Still, I'll tell you what I know – or, I'd better say, what I think I know. Please bear that proviso ever in mind.'

MacNucator replenished their glasses before settling himself down deep in his armchair to relate to his client what he thought he knew of:

The Life of Algernon 'Perpetual' Motion

'Motion is a Fife name, I believe, and he seems to have been born with it, but it could scarcely have been more appropriate for someone of such an elusive, quicksilver temperament, apparently from his earliest years – one who has indeed been in perpetual motion all his life. It's not easy to separate the chameleon-like shifts, which he has constantly effected, from his innate propensity for lying; to establish, I mean, what parts he has really played upon life's stage and those which he has only invented. He

appears to have been born in Dundee, and has claimed to
some of my informants that his father was the Town Clerk
of Tayport. The truth seems to be that the elder Motion
was merely a bookkeeper in the office of that important
legal functionary.

'Algy was the spoilt and only child of elderly, doting
parents. He grew up believing that his every wish had the
implicit character of a command. But he was a wretched
and sickly little boy with an intractable bronchial weakness, which no doubt gave rise to his recurrent nightmares of suffocation or drowning in sludge. Treated as
a semi-invalid and isolated from companions of his own
age during his early years, he inevitably took badly to
the rough-and-tumble of school life and was despised
and bullied. His only defence lay in his ready tongue
and his sneering wit, and of course when he realized
their effectiveness he developed and perfected these not
very likeable traits. Algy early discovered that he could
humiliate his tormentors and render them objects of ridi-
cule simply by imitating them: not only their voices and
mannerisms but the inner qualities and propensities which
these expressed, so that they felt at times that he had
stolen their very souls, and to his surprise and delight
they became frightened of him and came to regard him
as someone uncanny, dangerous, of sinister, otherworldly
powers.

'Motion, for his part, began to believe in the image
of himself which he saw reflected in the fear of his
schoolmates. He came to suppose that he could inhabit,
he felt, the person of anyone he chose, and thus acquire
a deadly power over them that could not be withstood.
While he was still in his teens his swaggering insolence

had already grown well-nigh insupportable, as he was progressively and self-destructively carried away by the ascendancy which he had – almost, as it seemed, without effort – acquired over those before whom, only brief months before, he had cowered and pleaded.

'But as his capacity to play parts, to imitate and impersonate, swelled and inflated, so did his sense – never strong – of his own self wither and atrophy. Apart from this one ambivalent gift his natural capacities were at best mediocre, but the deceiving sense of power into which he had grown convinced him that he had, you might say, a natural right to excel at anything to which he might turn his hand. Whenever he failed at any task, which happened frequently, he therefore refused point-blank either to accept the evidence or to draw the correct conclusion. Or, to put it more exactly, he was clearly unable to draw any conclusion from evidence which he refused to accept. We observe, then, the inexorable process by which Algernon Motion came to believe himself a universal genius and was obliged to attribute his failures to the misunderstanding and malice of others. He became, in short, a man with a grudge against the world.

'Algy fails to get into university because his maths are not good enough. He simply cannot pass the necessary exams. Yet he sincerely believes that he has, from a very early age, manifested an extraordinary natural aptitude for painting, drawing, music and scientific invention. He is convinced that he can enter the minds of artists, scientists and inventors, that he can emulate what in reality he can only imitate. He can act, sing, debate, paint reproductions of old masters, write popular songs, invent coffee-making machines. But no-one wants to know. Because he is an autodidact, and his only higher education has been acquired at evening classes, he is not taken seriously: he is the victim of invincible prejudice. His paintings remain unsold, his poems and songs unread, his patent applications are rejected. Corporate blindness thwarts him at every turn. All he has to show for his prolific artistry and invention, and his doggedly persistent pestering of the famous and influential, is a signed photograph of Marianne Faithfull, which becomes his most treasured possession.

'All this time he has been maintaining himself by lowly clerical work and menial or semi-skilled factory employment. But he is attractive to women and goes through a number of stormily unsatisfactory relationships. A masochistic warp in his nature gives rise to a pleasure in seeing his women with others, and he turns this perversion to commercial advantage by going in for a bit of pimping on the side. Somewhere along the way he becomes involved with the pathetic and disreputable person who now goes by the name of Mrs Motion. She is uncritically devoted to him and he exerts over her an unqualified dominance, reducing her to the condition of a devoted sex slave to himself and a professional provider to the lusts of others.

'Such was the squalid and worthless life of our Mr Algernon Motion when he fell in with an older and shrewder character who was considerably more experienced in fraudulent schemes. Jake "Opportunity" Knox had ducked and dodged around the fringes of criminality for long enough without ever hitting the big time. He wasn't slow, though, to recognize the potential in Algy's one genuine talent. An impersonator is an asset of inestimable value wherever fraud and deceit are one's business.

Motion had starred in *The Pirates of Penzance* as a schoolboy and indulged in a bit of amateur dramatics and even taken a few evening classes in acting, but he had never been on the professional stage. He was a natural, all the same. But he was not really interested in drama for its own sake; what attracted him to impersonation was the power it gave him over others, and especially the power to unsettle and to wound.

'From impersonation to imposture is of course but a very short step. "Opportunity" Knox and "Perpetual" Motion established over a few years an extremely profitable little business specializing in insurance fraud. I won't bore you with the details of all that, though they're of considerable professional interest to myself. But from what I can gather the Sinister Cabaret was originally set up as a sort of front for these rather complicated illegal activities. And in various ways it put Motion in touch with a range of people who were vulnerable to his charms and his predations. Eventually Knox died and the joint venture came to an end, but by that time Motion was quite a wealthy man. The business side of things was never his long suit, and he now continued with his impostures and his trickeries only for the sadistic pleasure and the sense of power which he derived from them. He had learned, you see, how to target those who were spiritually most at risk, and he came over the years to hone the Sinister Cabaret into an instrument of psychological terror by means of which he wore down the resistance of his victims, and even their will to live.

'You would be surprised at the great number of these unfortunates, and at how many prominent, successful and intelligent people he has succeeded in duping. So far as

I'm aware he has never killed anyone himself, but I know that he has been indirectly responsible for the deaths of several who have taken their own lives, believing themselves to be betrayed, disgraced, ruined or even mad. You have told me of one such instance yourself. Don't imagine for an instant that Mrs Henn-Harrier's death was an accident. She threw herself down Breakneck Corridor in the bitterness of jealousy and unrequited love. Oh, yes. I have made it my business to find out. That unhappy lady was desperately in love with the man she believed to be Colonel Gerald Beaglehowl, and had been for years. Ben Despair Lodge was a seething hell of sexual torment as poor deluded Maudie vied vainly (yet with undying hope!) with her dear friend Moira for possession of the cruel impostor. By an ingenious trick he arranged for her to discover, as she believed, that the person of the brave and dashing Colonel concealed the multiple and shifting identity of the Graf vom und zum Bagelhaul. That was the final straw, and I am afraid that after that she no longer wished to live.

'All this no doubt sounds very disheartening to you, Donald, as you prepare for your final showdown with Motion and the Cabaret. But the reality is that Motion is now a dying force. After so many years of impersonation and imposture his sense of himself has become so weak that he can scarcely be said to exist in the usual way. Because you have withstood all the terrors he has set up for you along the road, he is now in a real sense more vulnerable to you than you to him. He needs success, you see, to feed his faltering sense of his own reality, and with you full success has been eluding him. Self-doubt has now begun gnawing at his entrails. This performance next week will be his last great effort: already he suspects that he is severely, perhaps fatally, wounded. But don't mistake me, you mustn't let your guard drop. Remember that some of his henchmen may in the end prove tougher customers than Motion himself.

'Well, that's the story of our friend's life so far as I've been able to put it all together. But, of course, someone else might tell it quite differently.'

15

Retribution

The day arrived when the Sinister Cabaret were to perform in the village hall at Cul an Duirn.

Donald was very nervous. More, he was shit-scared. In spite of MacNucator's well meant support and reassurances, he would have given his right arm not to have had to face this ordeal. But he knew in his heart of hearts that there could be no ducking out of it: he had to be there. The detective assured him that he had been through much worse already. His experiences in the underground city had fortified him, renewed his inner resources, weakened the Cabaret's hold over him, and so on. But it is all very well, Donald was thinking a little resentfully, to talk in that sort of way when it's not you they're after. When you've had direct personal experience of such victimization there's little comfort to be derived from psychobabble.

How could he ever forget Motion's insinuating, contemptuous smile as he told the frantic Donald that Madeleine was asleep upstairs? Or recall without nausea the nightmare of the wife's lascivious, barefaced suggestiveness? How could he face yet again the dull malice at the back of Cant's eyes, deader than a fish on a slab? How, above all, could he bear to see once more that dreadful, taunting simulacrum of the wife he loved, identical to her in every feature and detail but lacking that indefinable something within, which animates and gives life?

Unthinkable, all of it!

Yet all of it had to be confronted. There was no going back.

In truth Peter understood very well just what Donald was feeling. But he refused to give him any advice: the outcome would emerge from the living moment. Nothing about this night could be predicted, directed or foreseen. The detective was at his side, yet Donald was on his own; he made this clear to him. But as they walked the two or three hundred yards down to the village hall it began to look as if Donald would not be lacking supporters. The whole village was turning out – theatrical evenings were after all a rarity in Cul an Duirn, and even the Sinister Cabaret qualified as an event.

And prominent among the throng were, of course, the denizens of the Mountain Dew.

They seemed to realize that this was a time of trial for the visitor they had taken to their communal heart, and their greetings were pointedly friendly and had an air of encouragement. Kenny Squeezebox, Arkady Vasilyevich Pachydermatov, Ingibjorg Sigursdottir, Big Hieronymus, even the Duck's-Arse-hairstyle man in the bottle-green suit – they were all there to express their solidarity. Kenny

Squeezebox was heading for the door with his jaw thrust out and a look of enormous determination on his face, his heels thumping down as if he had a quarrel with the pavement. Arkady Vasilyevich even came up and laid a huge Slavonic hand on Donald's shoulder.

'My friend!' he mumbled in a breaking voice, and was immediately overcome by emotion.

In front of the hall stood a decrepit old bus with the legend THE SINISTER CABARET clumsily painted in red along its side. The bus was grey with filth, and under the rear window someone had written with a finger in the dirt:

'A dog is for life – not just for Friday night.'

Not very nice, really; but then that's demotic wit, isn't it? Often not very nice. Whether or not it was one of the cast who had written it, the vulgar crudity of this witticism seemed somehow to typify the moral degeneracy of the Cabaret's perspective.

The seats in the hall were uncomfortable and the heating was not working properly. The show was late in starting, and behind the curtain there were thuds, scrapings and bangings as props were moved clumsily and hastily around, while raised voices could be heard in angry remonstrations. The audience was becoming restive. How unlike the deaf-mutes, Donald thought, for whom the wretched Cabaret could do no wrong! Tonight they might be in for a surprise. Just how big a surprise they were in for, however, even Donald could not have anticipated.

Eventually the curtain rose and Motion strode on stage in his canary-yellow waistcoat, his top hat and boots, and flourishing, as usual, his lion-tamer's whip. He at once launched into one of his silly verses, which he seemed to think so pungent and full of esoteric significance:

Raise high your expectations –
Come into the garden, Maud!
The adders are under the bushes,
The demons are abroad.

His usual arrogant confidence was lacking, though, and he even stumbled over the last line, saying 'aboard' instead of 'abroad', and then compounding his error by going back to correct it. Was the fatal self-doubt of which the detective had spoken manifesting itself already? The company went through some of the routines they had done for their earlier performance; there was an inertness in their delivery and at the same time an almost palpable anxiety, a consciousness that things were already not going well and could probably only get worse, and that the audience, this time, was not on their side. Not that there had so far been any protests. Instead there was an ominous silence in the hall: it was as if the people of Cul an Duirn were biding their time.

About fifteen minutes into the performance the moment Donald had been especially dreading arrived. The Madeleine figure was led on to the stage by Motion – on all-fours, on a lead, with a collar round her neck. He paraded her up and down for a minute or two without saying anything, then spoke some stupid verse which he articulated so badly that Donald could not make it out clearly, though it all hinged on the idea:

'Steal your wife . . . steal your life.'

Donald's terror dropped away from him; it was so painfully obvious to him now that the figure supposed to be his wife, though a masterpiece of verisimilitude, was patently not Madeleine but only a contemptible simulacrum.

In fact he felt almost embarrassed for the Sinister Cabaret, embarrassed for their ineptitude. He groaned aloud, a groan not of pain or fear but of contempt. This was the cue the audience had been waiting for. Some of them began to hiss, gently at first but with unmistakable menace. The actors became increasingly upset and confused and began fluffing their lines, stumbling and banging into each other. Only Cant, Donald noticed, appeared to be angry. The rest – even and perhaps especially Motion – were running scared.

The turning-point came when Motion, struggling to reassert his authority, stepped forward manfully to introduce a further skit with the lines:

Something's got to happen soon,
Something's got to give.
Space is just a macaroon
And Time is but a sieve.

He paused for a moment as if seeking to dominate the groundlings beneath him with the commanding force of his personality. Right bang in what should have been the centre of that imperious pause, a voice spoke out with absolute decision:

'This is *shite!*' It was Hector, the man from the Mountain Dew in the bottle-green suit. Though a sufferer from severe Brain Cell Deficit Disorder (BCDD), he knew shite when he saw it. Immediately someone threw a sweet-and-sour Chinese takeaway which caught Big

Scrote full on the face just as he was making his entry. And then the audience stormed the stage.

The first member of the Cabaret to react was Mrs Motion. She grabbed hold of a placard bearing some piece of Brechtian instruction to the audience on how to comport themselves ('Stop gaping so romantically', or something like that – why shouldn't they if they'd paid their money and that was what they wanted to do?), and let fly with it at Ingibjorg Sigurdsdottir. That substantial lady dodged it without difficulty, and before the Motion woman had time to recover herself delivered in return a practised two-finger poke in the eyes, to such remarkable effect that both eyes jumped out of their sockets and hung, still attached by various strings and filaments, bouncing on her cheeks. Now getting all kinds of confusing visual signals, and staggering all over the stage in her disorientation, she eventually fell off the edge and was trampled underfoot.

Mayhem was now let loose.

Donald had hung back at first as the audience rushed the stage, for he had always disdained being part of a mob; but when he saw the hated pseudo-Madeleine up there, cowering towards Cant for protection, he was seized with implacable, vengeful fury, and darted off to seize her by the arm and confront her with her imposture. But as soon as he laid his hand on her the flesh changed its texture beneath his touch and she was transformed instantaneously into a lifeless rag-doll. He was still gaping, the mammet dangling by the arm from his hand, when Cant came at him with a knife. He managed to leap backwards, thus saving his life, but felt a searing pain as he received a long, curving wound from the sternum down across his upper abdomen, which gushed blood through his sliced shirt.

Cant would have struck again, but just at that moment the dead body of Scrote fell heavily against him, knocking him to the ground and dislodging the knife from his grasp. Donald put his foot on the knife and Cant jumped to his feet and darted off through the wings. Scrote had been wielding a chair when Arkady Vasilyevich went in with the heid, administering such a butt to Scrote's forehead that his skull cracked like a walnut. The audience quickly overpowered the Cabaret; there were, of course, many more of the assailants. Motion was now getting a taste of his own whip as he cowered on the floor of the stage, pleading and blubbering.

Soon a cry went up:

'To the slurry pit with him!'

'Yes, to the slurry pit!'

Everyone began to stream out of the hall, Motion frog-marched in their midst.

'The up-endfulness of the esteemed and ridiculous Mr Motion is the proper caper, as Hurree Jamset Ram Singh might have remarked,' Donald managed to joke, as he attempted ineffectually to stanch his wound with his handkerchief.

'We'll have to get you to Dr Conradi soon,' said the detective, looking worried. He had taken no part in the attack on the Cabaret, and now appeared preoccupied, even distracted.

'Oh, I'll be all right, it's only superficial,' Donald hastened to reassure him. There suddenly flashed through Donald's mind Peter's warning against dealing with the Cabaret on their own terms: but he was completely caught up in the excitement and euphoria of the moment and dismissed the thought out of hand.

So with a lot of raucous shouting and merriment they all trouped out to the communal slurry pit, where Motion, now too weak to struggle, was duly up-ended and plunged headfirst in the slurry. Kenny Squeezebox and Big Hieronymus held him up by the knees, and for some little time his brightly polished boots with the spurs continued to kick. Then the kicks became feebler and finally subsided into mere twitches. One could almost have felt sorry for those boots.

Cant, who appeared to have escaped, was now the only member of the Sinister Cabaret left alive. It might seem rather an extreme reaction to a poor theatrical performance, but that's the way they do things in Cul an Duirn.

And it was really quite fortunate that Dr Conradi was in the village for the show: tending to Donald's wound made it a slightly less wasted evening for the good doctor. He was able to confirm that the wound had not penetrated deep enough to do any internal damage, but it was still a pretty nasty gash. He cleaned it all up and, his single eye gleaming with concentration, inserted half a dozen stitches. Donald had lost a bit of blood and felt slightly faint from shock, but his relief at the near elimination of the Cabaret buoyed him up almost to the point of euphoria. Dr Conradi advised him to go home to bed, but, no, Donald would not hear of it. He was going to the Mountain Dew to celebrate with the others.

Outside the village hall the Sinister Cabaret's disgusting old bus was now ablaze. The corpses, costumes, accoutrements and props had all been thrown in before it was dowsed with paraffin and torched. It was, as it happened, just about Guy Fawkes Night, but that celebration was unheard of in Cul an Duirn and this was no more than a happy coincidence. As the flames died down and the bus lay reduced to a twisted metal carcass, everyone tired quickly of this scene and all repaired to the Mountain Dew.

'Drinks on the house tonight!' shouted Kenny Squeezebox, and a tremendous carousal commenced. But tonight there was no aggro: instead they were all vying with each other in mutual compliments about their deportment during the recent engagement.

'It was you that started it all, Hector boy!' said someone, slapping the man in the bottle-green suit on the back, 'when you told them it was all *shite!*'

'Ach, that was nothing, boy. That was a right good whack Arkady Vasilyevich put into the boy, though, right enough!'

'I fancied that yellow waistcoat, myself. Anyone take it off him? It would need a right good wash, though, right enough!'

Motion's whip was now proudly displayed behind the bar as a trophy of the famous victory.

'He'll not be cracking that again in a hurry!' somebody observed.

And many other similarly unnecessary comments were passed.

The poster announcing the appearance of the Sinister Cabaret was ceremoniously ripped down and Kenny Squeezebox held it up and tore it up into neat squares, then removed it to the Gentlemen's Toilet, a place into which, before Donald's arrival, few gentlemen had ever penetrated. After that he got out his squeezebox, Big Hieronymus took his place behind the bar, Ingibjorg

Sigurdsdottir sang an unconscionably long Icelandic bal-
lad about another famous and no doubt equally bloody
victory in the days of the Sagas, and in short there was
a ceilidh and everybody got drunk. At some point it
occurred to someone to shout out that MacNucator should
go home for his fiddle; but he had already disappeared
without a word.

What Dreams May Come

16

Going Home

The next day was devoted to nursing a hangover and the one following to taking pleasure in its departure; so it was not until the third day after the rout of the Sinister Cabaret that Donald was forced to turn his mind to the matter of his own departure. It seemed to him clear that his business at Cul an Duirn was at an end, yet he felt curiously reluctant to leave. He had come to feel very much at home here, and now that he was relatively free from anxiety he wanted to savour the moment and give himself a decent respite from the exigencies of normal life. Yet he knew that his holiday, if such it could be called, had lasted quite long enough — though he had quite lost count of just how many days had passed since he had set off from Edinburgh on what he had thought of as a routine little break.

Madeleine, whom of course he had still not been able to contact, must be getting worried by now. But that was part of the trouble. He really didn't know quite how he was going to explain his extended absence, or begin to describe all the extraordinary things that had happened to him. He didn't want Madeleine to laugh in his face; yet what could he tell her but the unvarnished truth? If he didn't, she would no doubt draw her own conclusions and undoubtedly come up with the wrong answer. If he did, was it in the least likely that she would be able to accept his story? Madeleine was not jealous by nature; but in the absence of any immediately satisfactory explanation, wasn't it inevitable that she would suspect an affair? And how would he be able to disprove it? Who would be able to vouch for him? It was all quite worrying.

He put his concerns, naturally, to MacNucator. But Peter didn't seem to be his usual self; and in spite of his own euphoria Donald was uncomfortably aware that, strange to say, his mentor had seemed out of sorts ever since that climactic night.

'That's the least of your worries . . . ' the detective muttered, as if thinking aloud.

Then he seemed to recollect himself.

'Don't put your mind to it at all,' he advised. 'Put the idea of any preconceived plan of action completely out of your head. It will all work out completely differently from any way you can now imagine. Just like it did the other night. Believe me, Donald – I know what I'm talking about. I've had a lot of experience of cases of this sort. I'll give you a rough idea of the route you should take to get back to your car – just the beginning of the journey – and the rest will follow on. You just have to rely on your inner resources; and those are certainly in better shape than when you arrived here. But you must remain on your guard. Remember that Cant got away.'

He gazed out of the window with abstracted, narrowed eyes. Peter's mood was puzzling; but for all his little worries about Madeleine, Donald was possessed by an unquenchable optimism and good humour.

'Now. How much do I owe you, Peter, for everything you've done for me?'

'One bottle of Bruichladdich.' The detective responded with such promptitude that it was clear that he had been expecting this question to come next.

Donald's mouth fell open: he had really been thinking in terms of a four-figure sum at the least. He made and redoubled all the necessary protestations, but to no avail. One bottle of Bruichladdich was absolutely all that MacNucator wanted.

'Don't even mention my name to your friends,' he cautioned with a half-smile. 'You know I really am trying to retire.'

For all sorts of reasons it was not desirable, the detective said, for Donald to take the route back by which he had come. The one road which passed through Cul an Duirn was uselessly roundabout for his destination; which confirmed the information given him at the outset of his walk by Mr Chisholm. He would be better walking by the coast then cutting inland after about fifteen miles. There was a coastal track, but as Cul an Duirn stood on the north side of a promontory it would be sensible to cross this overland and pick up the path at the head of the sea loch which lay on its south shore. This way was over rough ground and MacNucator insisted on accompanying Donald that far to take him by the best route.

They left as soon as it was light, on a raw November morning. Donald had said goodbye to his friends at the

Mountain Dew the night before. The pair walked in virtual silence for an hour or more, picking their way through a rocky landscape of dead bracken and sparse heather interspersed with difficult boggy patches. When they reached the crest of the promontory and looked down on the narrow, fjord-like sea loch stretched below them in the chill, grey morning, they halted for a brief rest.

'There's one thing I should warn you about,' said Peter, gazing broodingly into the barren distances. 'You have probably not seen the last of Cant. He seems to have got away that night, and he's not the type that gives up easily. What's more, he will have vengeance in his heart. So be watchful.'

'That's all right,' said Donald. 'I've got vengeance in my heart too, and with better reason than him. I'll be ready for him.' Since the rout of the Sinister Cabaret he had felt extraordinarily energized, full of hope and renewed vitality.

'Deal with him as you must,' said Peter. 'I can't say any more than that.'

'Don't worry.'

After a short rest they trudged on, down the south-facing slope of the promontory and heading east towards the head of the loch. The track which Donald was to take was already visible, twisting along by the opposite shore. They were scrambling down a steep rocky descent and Donald, who had no head for heights, was in danger of freezing from his extreme fear of falling, when Peter, who was ahead, suddenly stopped in his tracks, crouched forward instinctively, and, motioning Donald to stay where he was, pointed silently down at the loch.

Donald gasped aloud at the sight which met his eyes.

174

Where the loch narrowed towards its head a sea-serpent had just surfaced. It was swimming so swiftly and with such awe-inspiring power that he thought it must have emerged from some underwater cave or passageway to have got up such a head of steam. As more of its body appeared on the surface it was seen to be of great length and size, not humped but rugged, dragon-like, horny-skinned. Then a second beast surfaced, and then a third; they moved with almost magical swiftness and with majestic power. The first had a reptilian head, the second that of a horse, while the head of the third, which at first struck him as bear-like, seemed as it drew closer to have a quasi-human quality, like a Sphinx. The travellers watched in utter silence as the three creatures passed below them, experiencing, each within himself, an access of numinous terror and awe. With extraordinary rapidity the three beasts surged out of the loch and into the open sea, and were soon no more than specks on the horizon.

MacNucator turned to Donald, his face pale and strange; unfathomable. No word passed his lips but it was as if he said, 'There – you see!' As for Donald, he was beyond speech, but as they set off again down the perilous slope he felt miraculously re-energized and completely freed from his terror of falling, possessed in the depths of his being by the wonder of life.

Within half an hour they had reached the track at the head of the loch, where the strange detective must leave his friend and return by the way he had come.

'You know that I can't find the words to thank you,' said Donald. 'Where do I leave the coast and head inland?'

'You'll know when you get there. It wouldn't make any sense if I tried to explain it now. When the moment comes you'll see that there's really only one thing you can do . . . Nothing is easy, Donald. But whatever happens, hang on to your hope. Never despair.'

Donald frowned; but saw that he would have to make do with this cryptic reply. It was not very satisfactory – even a little ominous; but when they had parted and he was journeying on alone he felt somehow that his friend was still with him, but within, and that he would continue to live and act under the inexplicable detective's tutelage and protection.

As he trudged along the south shore of the sea loch, Donald kept his eyes peeled for any sight of the three sea monsters, but nothing broke the monotony of the grey, endless waves. Towards the mouth of the loch the path began to climb steeply to bypass the headland and follow the line of the cliffs (home to tens of thousands of nesting kittiwakes) above the shore facing the open sea. On a clear day there should have been magnificent views from up here, but it was still raw and overcast and beginning to drizzle. Donald had no idea where this journey was to take him and he was alone for the first time in many days. In such circumstances it would not have been surprising if he had been depressed and gloomy, yet this was not the case. On the contrary, he felt at once calm and vigorous, and ready to encounter whatever dangers might yet lie in his path. Partly this was because he knew that the Sinister Cabaret had been not only neutralized but dismembered; but he dated his inner confidence more particularly from the vision of the sea monsters.

He had been walking for perhaps an hour on the path above the cliffs, surrounded by the clamourings of innumerable sea birds, when he saw ahead of him a curious natural formation. A great dome of rock rose out of the cliff immediately before him, enclosing a cave or grotto into which the path led. The rock threw out a buttress wall to the left of the track also, like a protecting arm. All at once a figure stepped out of the shadows of the cavern and stood in the middle of the track with its arms folded.

It was Cant.

His stance was identical to that which he had adopted on the school drive close on fifty years before; and, as on that occasion, Donald could only continue walking, slowly, towards him.

Cant had chosen his place well. To Donald's right the cliffs dropped three hundred feet to the rocky shore; to his left was the steep buttress of rock. He would not turn and flee. Cant unfolded his arms and stood with the knife in his hand. It was the same knife he had wielded on the last night of the Cabaret, which had etched the wound on Donald's stomach and which the latter had put his foot on when it had fallen from the assailant's hand: how had he retrieved it?

No matter.

As he continued advancing slowly towards his lifelong enemy, Donald remembered how he had gained a brief respite on a previous occasion by doing something quite unexpected. This time he was not in a position to do the same thing, but perhaps he could do something equally unlooked for. He smiled.

Clearly nonplussed, Cant frowned.

Still smiling sweetly, Donald pointed just over Cant's right shoulder and nodded as if towards something he had just noticed over there. Cant shouldn't have been taken in, of course, and his loss of full attention lasted only a split second, but in that instant he received a boot in the crotch which doubled him up in gasping agony, and the knife clattered uselessly on the stones. Donald gave him a great shove and then simply shouldered him off the edge. Cant threw out his arms and legs as he fell, then pulled them back in again as a great projection of rock, of wicked sharpness, rushed up to meet him. Ripped apart, he balanced on it precariously for an instant then plunged again, out of Donald's sight, into the distantly sounding depths.

Donald kicked the knife over after him.

That dealt with, Donald peered a little apprehensively into the interior of the cave. There was no doubt that this was where the track led: this must be what MacNucator had been referring to when he had said that it would be clear what Donald must do when the time came. So here was another testing time ahead of him. He took off his backpack, leaned against a boulder and ate his sandwiches. It would not be sensible to venture into the unknown on an empty stomach. Donald was more than a little prone to claustrophobia and the idea of groping his way for an unknown distance through a dark, damp cavern full of unthinkable hazards was not appealing. But he had done all right so far and he retained his faith in the detective's judgement. Peter would not have sent him this way if it had not been the best way.

After a short respite he shouldered his pack once more and moved cautiously into the cave. As far as the daylight penetrated, it seemed as if the path continued deep into the interior. The roof was at this point about twice his own height and the floor of the cavern some thirty feet wide. The walls were dampish and covered with some kind of moss or lichen which gave off a distinct, greenish luminosity. As he slowly advanced it became clear that this curious effulgence was just sufficient to keep the underground passageway from impenetrable darkness, even when no light from outside could any longer be penetrating within. The surface under his feet remained quite walkable, though often bumpy and a little slippery.

For reassurance he kept close to the left-hand wall, running his hand along it as he advanced. His footsteps made a hollow echo. He could never see more than a foot or two in front of him, but it was not becoming any darker. But what did worry Donald was the unmistakable impression he had that the corridor was very gradually narrowing and the roof coming down to meet his head. The atmosphere, too, was becoming damper and more unwholesome, almost fetid. His body was covered with a clammy sweat. He knew that he was in danger of giving way to panic: he had an impulse to turn and flee before it was too late. But something kept him doggedly advancing.

Before long he could no longer walk, even stooped: he had to get down on his hands and knees and crawl. He would have to abandon his backpack, and he took it off. The walls of the passageway were now bumping against his elbows. But still he pressed on, sweating and groaning. Soon he was flat on his stomach, propelling himself forward on his hands, inch by inch. It was now impossible for him to turn, nor could he any longer even have moved backwards. There was no sign of the passageway widening again, and he could now see barely anything. His wound had become agonizing, his shoulders were almost pinioned by the walls; he could scarcely breathe.

I am going to die here, he thought, *alone and helpless, utterly helpless and alone, unknown, forgotten by all.*

Yet he struggled on, moving now with the slow contractions of a worm. On and on and on. There seemed no end to the agony; he had lost all sense of time. He could not rest, his panic drove him on; a fixed condition of panic, which was a fearful but undeniable paradox. But at last he became aware of a vestigial lightening. He had known, after all, that this must happen. He strove towards it; heaven knows for how long. Eventually the light resolved itself into a definite point. The passageway began to widen again — he could get on to his knees; then all at once it opened into a chamber: dear God, he could stand! Not without great difficulty, it was true. He was all but finished. But the joy and relief in his heart could not be measured. He leaned, gasping, against the cave wall. His hand went to his wound: it had oozed and bled a bit but the stitches held. He could scarcely believe he was alive.

The source of the light was a hole in the roof of the cave, above the wall opposite the exit from the passageway. In fact it was where the slope of the roof merged with the wall, and so not impossibly high to reach. By piling a number of rocks lying about the floor of the cavern into a cairn, Donald was able to get his arms out of the aperture just far enough to gain some purchase with his elbows on the ground above. The hole was barely wide enough to admit his shoulders. Fortunately his arms were strong, and after a short, violent effort he succeeded in pulling himself out. To his astonishment he saw that it was already dark: the light which had guided him was that of an almost-full moon. He was lying on the floor of an eerie wood. No more than a hundred yards from where he was, the wood thinned out and ended; beyond it was a long, high wall. But he lay in utter exhaustion for perhaps half an hour before he felt able to move and investigate further.

Eventually Donald rose wearily to his feet. His clothes were torn and filthy and he had nothing with him at all. In spite of the season it was not cold. He walked out of the wood towards the wall, and followed it round a right-angled corner. At last he came upon a little wrought-iron gate and went in. He found himself in a walled garden of great beauty and symmetry. Immaculate lawns were criss-crossed by paths and interspersed with borders set in intricate patterns. The moon's platinum light and the utter stillness and quiet of the deserted garden imparted to the scene an almost ethereal quality which pulled at his heart. For several minutes he stood silently, rapt in wonder, then he moved slowly through the garden.

From a long way away came a faint but unmistakable sound of music; then he became aware of the dim shape of a large building set on a rise, at a considerable distance beyond the walled garden. Emerging from a gate identical to that by which he had come in, Donald began to walk through wooded parkland towards the big house, which he could now see was lit from many windows, though mostly their light was dimmed by curtains. The music grew more distinct as he came nearer – dance music: it seemed that a ball was in progress.

Donald approached the vast mansion almost in a trance. Noise, laughter and music drew him on and he found himself tip-toeing up to the windows of the ballroom. Someone had pulled a curtain back and thrown open one of the windows, and he cautiously keeked inside. A great company were dancing, many others standing watching, with glasses in their hands. The exquisite women were in long flowing gowns, the men in full evening dress: the scene was one of unmatched opulence. It seemed to be the last waltz.

Donald's attention fastened on an elderly couple – most of the dancers were quite young – who were pirouetting around the dance floor with extraordinary, old-fashioned grace. They seemed to have caught the gaze of many of the onlookers, too; and gradually the other dancers left the floor, as it were in homage to the old couple, until they were the only dancers left on the floor. Round and round they went in tireless harmony, a glow of warmth and love lighting up their faces. The elderly couple were Donald and Madeleine, twenty years on. In spite of her years, Madeleine still seemed to him very beautiful.

'Relics of a bygone age,' remarked a young man standing near the window to the woman beside him.

'Yes – but what a *lovely* old couple!' she replied.

'Oh, yes, a lovely old couple,' said the man.

At last the waltz came to an end and the company joined together in 'Auld Lang Syne'. Donald moved away from the window and round a corner of the building until he came upon a little recess where he could skulk unobserved. He could not imagine what would happen if he were to be discovered there in his utterly disreputable condition. It was quite some time before the merrymakers began to trickle out of various doors, talking and laughing loudly and boisterously and shouting prolonged goodbyes. Some got into cars and roared off, others were driven away in the taxis which had been gliding up the drive for some time. It must have been well over an hour before the last cars drove off and things began to quieten down. There were still voices to be heard from within, though; presumably some of the company were staying overnight.

On a rash impulse which he could not account for, Donald found a side entrance and entered the house; immediately opposite the door was a staircase and he went up it. He walked along a vast corridor and passed several people obviously making for bed, but oddly enough no-one paid him the slightest attention. There were lights under the doors on this corridor and some of the people went into their bedrooms. Coming to another staircase at the far end, Donald ascended once more and found this higher floor quiet and deserted, lit only by a single light a long way off. Seeing a door with no light under it, he turned the handle very cautiously and went in. The room appeared to be empty and he turned the light on. A bed was beautifully made up and everything fresh and tidy, but there was no sign of any personal possessions or anything else to indicate present habitation. The room looked vaguely familiar, but Donald was far too tired to pursue the idea. Utterly exhausted, he threw his clothes off, turned out the light, got into bed and was asleep on the instant.

17

Mr Cant

Donald awoke in the morning restored and invigorated. He stretched luxuriously and looked around him. At first he was not clear where he was, but then the events of the previous day came back to him with the utmost clarity. To his astonishment he saw that his tattered and filthy clothes had been removed during the night and replaced by a completely new set of similar type. But there was something else odd. The feeling that he had had before he went to bed, that this room was slightly familiar, returned to him; and now he thought he remembered what it reminded him of. But the room he associated with it had been unfurnished. A little alarmed, he got out of bed and went to the window. What he had begun to suspect was true. He was in the room in which he had spent the night before he set out on his hike to Cul an Duirn – the room in Cant's Hotel!

But Donald was becoming used to surprises and he

decided to go with the flow. He went into the bathroom and found that washing things, including a toothbrush and toothpaste, had been made ready for him. He took a hot shower and dressed. It was about 8.30 and he was ravenously hungry. It was clear as he went downstairs that the renovation which had been in progress during his previous visit was now complete. As he passed the reception desk the girl behind it smiled in the friendliest manner.

'Good morning, Mr Humbie,' she said. 'I hope you slept well?' – just as if he had checked in the previous evening in the normal manner! He made his way through to the dining room and ordered a large cooked breakfast and coffee. Glancing again idly over the menu as he waited for his food to arrive, he noticed that it was headed 'The Stag's Breath Hotel'.

Cant, it seemed, had become a non-person very quickly.

The breakfast proved to be excellent. Donald was now in high good humour and anxious to be on his way. Fortunately his wallet had been transferred with contents intact from his old trousers to his new, so he settled his bill and went out into the village street. It was a bright, cold day with none of yesterday's dampness. He sauntered over to Mr Chisholm's shop, and there was his car parked outside just as he had left it. He went in to thank the old shopkeeper for his good service in pointing him towards Peter MacNucator.

Mr Chisholm seemed pleased to see him.

'I can't thank you enough for putting me in touch with Peter,' said Donald. 'He's transformed my situation, no doubt about that at all.'

Mr Chisholm nodded with satisfaction, as if to indicate

that he wouldn't have expected anything less. 'Ay, he's a good man Peter MacNucator, right enough. And are you on your way back home now? Well, drive carefully, Mr Humbie. There was quite a hard touch of frost last night. Winter's just around the corner.'

Donald was so full of exuberance and *joie de vivre* as he drove out of the village that he found himself breaking into song. He remembered the terrible state of mind he had been in when he had arrived – so long ago it seemed now. There was the place he had turned in to when he realized that he had in his panic been reversing down the road – what confusion he must have been in! And – yes, that was it – there was the half-grown-over forestry cutting he had darted into to give the pursuing Range Rover the slip.

And now he was descending the winding route towards the main road and familiar, reassuring territory. By evening he should be back at home with Madeleine.

He was just thinking that perhaps as he passed through Fliuchary he would call in at Tigh-na-Coille to check that Mrs Macrae was all right, when he pulled into the main road virtually without looking to his right. He was just aware of a huge shape looming over his shoulder and then there was a ferocious impact and he felt himself go through the windscreen. Then he was skiting – it seemed to him quite slowly – across the surface of the road, in horrendous pain, thinking three thoughts simultaneously: 'This is it, this is the end – how did I forget my seat-belt? – what a crazy way to go after all I've survived!' After that came a sensation of total paralysis, and he seemed to be sucked down a dark tunnel, disappearing into a vortex, falling, falling, plunging, with a great surging and singing in his ears which became louder and louder . . .

There came a kind of jolt and he found himself lying in a bed. He lay there for quite a long time, vaguely aware of a mutter of low voices close by. There seemed no good reason to do anything. Eventually he decided to open his eyes. Two dim figures seemed to be bending towards him. But his thoughts were still directed inwards. Everything that had happened to him from the time he left home was simultaneously present to his mind, and with extraordinary clarity. He laughed inwardly and tried to shake his head.

'And if you know what that was all about, you're a better man than I am, Gunga Din!' he muttered to himself.

'He must have been dreaming,' he heard one of the voices say. And then the other spoke much more loudly and purposively:

'Can you hear me, Donald? It's me! You gave us a fright! But you're round the corner now – you're going to be all right.'

The voice was Madeleine's, there was no doubt of that. He felt her hand on his right arm. He opened his eyes again. Yes, there was Madeleine looking down at him and smiling tenderly, and he could see that there were tears in her eyes. The other person, he saw, was a nurse. He realized that he was in hospital, probably in a side-ward. The light seemed rather dim. He tried to smile back at Madeleine, to let her know that he was happy that she was there, but he wasn't sure if he had succeeded. There were tubes coming out of his right arm, contraptions round about him; for some reason he was reminded of a spider's web. With his left hand he tried to feel his body for damage. He was relieved to find that he could move it. The crash was horrifically vivid in his memory. His head ached badly, but oddly enough the only place where he could find anything definitely amiss was where Cant had carved the wound in his abdomen: there was a big dressing there. It must have opened up as he was propelled across the road. There was something nagging at his mind.

'Was anyone else hurt?' he whispered.

Madeleine looked puzzled. 'How? What do you mean, darling?'

'In the crash.'

'The crash? What crash?'

'The one that landed me in here, of course,' he managed to say, with great difficulty. Madeleine opened her mouth to speak then closed it again and looked with raised eyebrows at the nurse, who returned her glance but remained impassive.

'Don't worry about anything just now, Donald,' said Madeleine. 'Just concentrate on getting better.'

Donald closed his eyes again wearily. He realized that he had come very close to death. He wanted to run over the events of his journey again before they became irremediably blurred and confused, as they were already beginning to do. He thought again about Queenie, and the way she had looked back at him before she plunged into the deeps and he shot away from her to the surface of the waters. He thought about her with love, but this time without pain. He said to himself that this journey had been to equip him better for that other journey which he, like all of us, would some day have to make. He opened his eyes again but the lids threatened to droop back.

'You're tired, dear,' said Madeleine, and stroked his arm.

'The surgeon will be coming to have a look at him in just a minute,' said the nurse.

Madeleine raised her hand and, in a familiar gesture, felt the back of her neck under her luxuriant hair. 'Oh! Yes . . . well, in that case I'd better be getting off,' she said, and looked towards the door; but she seemed reluctant to go, and stood twisting and turning her handbag over in her hands. Just then a white-coated figure appeared in the room and stood at the foot of the bed with folded arms. And Donald saw Madeleine's face light up unexpectedly when she saw the surgeon, in a way he had not known it do for a long time.

'Well! . . . Here's Mr Cant now!' she cried, almost excitedly.

And Donald, remembering all too clearly the detective's warning, began at once to marshal his flagging inner resources, in silent preparation for the struggle still to come.

Also by John Herdman

and available in paperback from

www.blackacebooks.com

Imelda, and other stories

What is the secret surrounding the birth of Imelda's child? This short but immensely rich and provocative novel presents us with two contradictory accounts of events which lead to madness and death for the scions of a genteel Border family. The reader is invited to decide which testimony, if either, is to be relied upon.

"This subtle, assured little masterpiece should go a long way towards placing him amongst our foremost writers." *Books in Scotland*.

£9.95 RRP. ISBN 0–7486–6140–9.

Ghostwriting

When Leonard Balmain is asked to "ghost" the autobiography of the mysterious Torquil Tod, he finds himself drawn into an unwanted complicity with the dark revelations unfolding within the story. When Tod's tale turns to murder and sexual betrayal, Leonard realizes he now knows too much and is in danger of ending up a dark secret himself.

"A dark, cautionary tale, utterly compelling and charged with Herdman's unwavering sense of irony and his sharp satirical bite . . . a writer very clearly on top of his craft, with wit, sub-tlety, and great panache." *Scotsman*.

£9.95 RRP. ISBN 0–7486–6211–1.

To order direct within UK, P&P free, send cheque for £10 per book. To order from outside UK, send sterling cheque for £15 (fifteen GBP) per book. To:

Black Ace Books, PO Box 6557
Forfar, DD8 2YS, Scotland